Dynasty smiled at Aaron, then frowned, puzzled by his expression. "What?" she asked.

"You look gorgeous. Why are you down here driving Rory nuts? Aren't I enough?"

Her body flushed from the ankles to eyebrows. "You talk like a fool."

"I feel like one too. Put me out of my misery."

"All right." She looked around her.

Aaron groaned. "You're looking for a shotgun, aren't you?"

She smirked. "You bet."

"Our children are going to be awful. I should warn my parents."

"Stop talking like that." She felt a rising desperation. He could make her love him. Losing him would be more devastating than anything that had happened to her in New York.

"Stop thinking about ways to get rid of me, Dynasty Jones." He reached for her and pulled her into his arms. "Dynasty," he said against her mouth. "I love your name."

Before she could reply, he'd slanted his mouth over hers, searching, questing.

WHAT ARE *LOVESWEPT* ROMANCES?

They are stories of true romance and touching emotion. We believe those two very important ingredients are constants in our highly sensual and very believable stories in the LOVE-SWEPT line. Our goal is to give you, the reader, stories of consistently high quality that may sometimes make you laugh, sometimes make you cry, but are always fresh and creative and contain many delightful surprises within their pages.

Most romance fans read an enormous number of books. Those they truly love, they keep. Others may be traded with friends and soon forgotten. We hope that each LOVESWEPT romance will be a treasure—a "keeper." We will always try to publish

LOVE STORIES YOU'LL NEVER FORGET
BY AUTHORS YOU'LL ALWAYS REMEMBER

The Editors

Loveswept ® 754

DYNASTY JONES

HELEN MITTERMEYER

BANTAM BOOKS

NEW YORK · TORONTO · LONDON · SYDNEY · AUCKLAND

DYNASTY JONES

A Bantam Book / September 1995

All rights reserved.
Copyright © 1995 by Helen Mittermeyer.
Back cover art copyright © by George Tsui.
Floral border by Joyce Kitchell.
No part of this book may be reproduced or transmitted in any
form or by any means, electronic or mechanical,
including photocopying, recording, or by any
information storage and retrieval system, without
permission in writing from the publisher.
For information address: Bantam Books.

If you would be interested in receiving protective vinyl covers for your
Loveswept books, please write to this address for information:

Loveswept
Bantam Books
P.O. Box 985
Hicksville, NY 11802

ISBN 0-553-44515-4

Published simultaneously in the United States and Canada

Bantam Books are published by Bantam Books, a division of Bantam Dou-
bleday Dell Publishing Group, Inc. Its trademark, consisting of the words
"Bantam Books" and the portrayal of a rooster, is Registered in U.S.
Patent and Trademark Office and in other countries. Marca Registrada.
Bantam Books, 1540 Broadway, New York, New York 10036.

PRINTED IN THE UNITED STATES OF AMERICA

OPM   0 9 8 7 6 5 4 3 2 1

PROLOGUE

Aaron Burcell had been to central New York State before. He'd been an undergrad at Cornell University some thirty miles south of Yokapa County. He'd enjoyed the deep gorges, the high waterfalls, beautiful Cayuga Lake. He'd no intention of returning, doing what his family had done for a century and a half, breeding and racing thoroughbreds.

This wasn't about a pleasure trip, however. He wanted to confront a woman named Dynasty Jones . . . about stealing a million-dollar racehorse. If the horse on her farm belonged to him, as Aaron's friend, Dex Beaman, believed, Aaron was more than willing to take whatever steps were necessary to get Moonstruck back to Kentucky. Dex had heard about a thoroughbred being boxed into a herd of mustangs. From the description, and it had come thirdhand to Dex, it could be the Burcell Farms horse that had disappeared several months back. Aaron had to check it out.

As he stared at the name on the mailbox, Honeysuckle Farm, Aaron inhaled the fragrance of the honeysuckle that lined the drive. The bushes ran along a split-rail fence that separated the narrow way from a small cottage, fronting on the highway. Did the cottage belong to the farm? he wondered. He looked down the long, rutted driveway to a house and a barn, partially shielded by pines over forty feet tall. Their whispering was the orchestra for the shrill screech of a soaring red-tailed hawk. Watching the graceful figure bank, stall, and climb, Aaron pondered what could take place in the next hour or so. Finding Moonstruck was all important.

There had been a lot of nasty business going on in thoroughbred racing. Owners had been charged with killing horses to collect their insurance. Other owners, Aaron had heard, arranged to have the thoroughbreds stolen and then killed. Some that were stolen, though, weren't killed. Supposedly those were hidden in small herds of lesser breeds, mustangs, job horses, even mules, then were sold to buyers at open country markets or auctions. Aaron found it hard to believe that any thoroughbred could be hidden in another herd. Still, the whole business was bizarre. That many special horses were killed and others spirited away to be handed over to designated black market buyers, was an anathema to him. That some of those could be right here in this country, infuriated him. Retattooed, their coats dyed, they were carted off to secret stud farms. They'd be kept long enough to impregnate some designated mares, then they'd be killed. Too risky to keep them. A knowledgeable horseman could spot a thoroughbred.

His grandfather had told him similar stories about his own early days as a horse buyer. Aaron had thought it would be impossible to pull off such stunts today.

He rubbed his neck. He could be on a wild-goose chase. Could even someone who didn't know horses, purchase a thoroughbred in a herd of mustangs and not know it? And was it just coincidental that the same purchaser had been involved in the infamous Boehrman-Dearman scandal a few years back? Dex had given Aaron chapter and verse about the successful stockbroker who'd beaten a charge of illegal trading. Had Dynasty Jones changed careers to become an underworld horse trader? Great plot for a dime detective tale.

The more Aaron ran it around his head, the more absurd it became. He was tempted to back out of the drive and return to Ithaca. His hand hovered over the gear shift.

Hell! He was there. The horse had been traced to this farm. Aaron put the rented Porsche in gear and started down the drive.

ONE

Popping sweat like a roasting piglet wasn't part of the plan, Dynasty thought. She had returned to Yokapa County to get away, kick back, change her scene, not work like a field hand from dawn to dusk. Get away? Kick back? Maybe hide out was a better description.

Dynasty inhaled a shaky breath and plunged her pitchfork into a bale of hay. She spread the hay out on the dirt floor of the painted aluminum barn. Its exterior was a little bent and rusted, but so what? It kept out the rain, refracted the sun on the hottest days, and didn't let a drop of snow or sleet into the stalls when the upper doors were closed. One bale to go and the stables would be done. They were cleaned first, then fresh hay was laid in every stall and the wide area in front. It was a daily chore, like eating breakfast. Two things she hadn't done in New York City—pitch hay and down oatmeal.

She exhaled and looked around the stable. It

would be ready for the six mustangs when they finished grazing on the upper pasture near the highway. Mustangs! What was she doing with them? She didn't know zip about horses. She'd been born at Sheppard Air Force Base in Wichita Falls, Texas, and left there at the tender age of three months for a variety of cities and bases around the world, wherever her career Air Force father was posted. She'd finished her education at Cornell, then had gone on to Harvard Business. Some short visits in the summer to her grandmother's farm had been her only exposure to agriculture and animal husbandry. Her grandmother had had mules and had raised oats and alfalfa. Now Dynasty had mustangs and grew gooseberries and blueberries. Good Lord!

"What're you thinking, Dynasty?"

Dynasty cocked her head, eyeing her partner in berry farming. "About insanity."

Dorothy pursed her lips. "Yours or mine?"

"Mine. What am I doing here? Finance is my field."

"Was. Now you're a farmer. Your grandmother would be pleased you're working this farm."

Dynasty closed her eyes for a moment.

"Forget the past," Dorothy whispered. "This is your life. If you run into any of those turncoat friends of yours, you can tell them to put the Dow where the sun don't shine. You're into berries now."

Dynasty's smile was twisted. "Yeah. Maybe if I'd done that at the beginning, instead of being so stunned at being charged I didn't react, I might've avoided . . ." Her voice drifted away. "Why talk about it? It's past. They're memories from hell, and I don't live there anymore."

"Right. I'll give the horses a little more grazing time while I get their mash ready." She chuckled. "They have a habit of nudging that could knock me clean over when they see the oat bag. They've started to gain weight and feistiness since their arrival."

"Something had to improve. It hasn't been the checkbook. I'm beginning to understand the phrase 'eat like a horse.' Maybe I'll try your miracle mix of water, oats, and whatever. I could use some of their energy."

Dorothy laughed. "Might work." She gazed around her. "Looks right nice in here."

"Thanks." Dynasty leaned on the pitchfork, puffing upward to get an errant curl off her forehead. She needed a hair cut. Bottom of the list. "The stable's cleaner than the house."

Dorothy pursed her lips. "Serves you right for hiring that Missy-messup. You'd've been better to hire Sarah Meistersaenger and—"

Dynasty shook her head. "We've been over this, Dorothy. Merrybelle was cheaper—"

"No 'count family, the Betterboles. Their place is a mess. Merrybelle is no shucks as a housekeeper. In fact she's as no count as her brother, Denby . . ." Dorothy's head whipped around, her nose wrinkling. "Car comin' up the drive."

Dynasty stared at the woman. Dorothy Lesser was in her fifties, widowed, with two children who were now in California. She'd lived in the small house at the beginning of the lane leading to Honeysuckle Farm for thirty years. She'd shown up at Dynasty's door the day Dynasty had moved in and announced her many capabilities. She hadn't overstated any of them, and Dynasty had never regretted hiring her. At the moment, though, she questioned Dorothy's observation. The farm was situated over a thousand feet from the highway.

"I don't hear . . ." Then she did. It didn't sound like a truck coming down the rut-filled driveway. Before winter she'd need to have a load of stone to fill the holes, otherwise she'd never be able to plow when the snow came.

Following Dorothy out of the barn, she turned left and stopped dead. A Porsche! Why? Who? She hadn't seen one since her late, unlamented stint on Wall Street.

A man, garbed like his transportation—top drawer—unfolded himself from the driver's seat. Pausing at the front of the sports car, he looked at her. "Dynasty Jones?"

She backed one step, fisting her hands. She didn't trust men like him, with that tall, sleek look of well-being. His hard planed face could've been chiseled from the finest New York cherry. A perfect palette for the deep green eyes. A well-toned body, as though he worked out in one of the outrageously expensive health clubs in Manhattan. Handball. Tennis. Golf at a select country club if business called for it. Sailing could be his forte. Yes, she knew the type. Enmity rose unbidden. Avoid the foe when he's unbeatable. She'd learned that the hard way.

Dorothy glanced from the man to Dynasty, puzzlement in her look.

Aware she'd kept everyone at bay, Dynasty nodded. "And you?"

"Aaron Burcell."

"What can—?"

"You from Burcell Farms in Kentucky?" Dorothy cut in, curiosity in every line of her body.

He nodded.

"You've had some Derby winners. Belmont Stakes. I saw your Kiltie Dea run in the Preakness, on television. Went like a streak."

Burcell smiled. "Great horse. Still is. Retired to stud and living like a king."

"Deserves it. Earned his keep," Dorothy said in her clipped way.

"I agree."

His smile was lightning, Dynasty thought. A scorcher. She backed another step. He'd picked up rays from the sun and turned them to electricity. Charmer! She'd known a few of those. "Sorry, Mr. Burcell. If you want to discuss blooded stock, this isn't the place. I'm too busy and don't know enough about the subject. So, if you'll excuse . . ." Her voice faded, her focus switching away from the hunk with the deep chestnut-hued hair to his car. Something was dripping from the undercarriage.

"I believe you have something that belongs to me," Burcell said.

"What? Your oil pan?" Dynasty asked, her eyes on the spreading pool under the Porsche.

He leaned back and looked down, catching the same drip-drip that she'd seen. "Damn!" He glared at her. "Why don't you get your driveway fixed?"

"Nobody invited you here." Dynasty glowered back, her ready temper coming to the fore. She'd taken plenty of crap from some Superfines on Wall Street. No more. Maybe he wasn't from the Street, but he was their clone. To blazes with him. This was her place.

She'd never thought to use her inheritance from Gramma Peabody. But then she'd never thought she'd change her life so drastically. She liked it, though. She'd sweated, fretted, and bled her small holding into producing the blueberries, raspberries, and gooseberries she and Dorothy carted to the Green Market in Manhattan, just under four hundred miles from the farm. She'd never figured that such a crop would support her and Dorothy, but it did. Not in great style, of course. She paid the bills, managed a luxury now and then. She put in ten- and fifteen-hour days tending the farm, managing the books, and playing housekeeper to six horses. She didn't make the megabucks that had once been hers, but she was doing all right. Keeping her head above water had been a struggle at first. She'd been incredibly proud when she'd managed a home improvement loan and gotten the bathroom fixed and the cistern repaired. She could shower and do her laundry. Next year, if the creek don't rise, as Dorothy was fond of saying, she'd overhaul the kitchen.

First, though, she had to get rid of the Suit.

He was staring at her. "Hospitable, aren't you?"

"Your manners are hammered in copper, are they, Mr. Burcell?"

Dorothy gasped.

"Look, Dynasty—"

"Ms. Jones to you."

Dorothy hiccuped.

Aaron Burcell moved a step closer, arms akimbo. "I didn't come here to fight with you—"

"How reassuring."

"Dynasty . . ." Dorothy whispered.

Dynasty subsided, biting her lip. "Go on."

"You have a horse of mine, I think, and—"

"Wrong. The ones on this farm are mine. Purchased by me. I have the bill of sale." She imitated him and slapped her hands on her hips, leaning forward on the balls of her feet. "Mustangs, Mr. Burcell. From the West. Brought here and sold at ridiculous prices because they were starving to death, or going to be turned into horse meat for the delectation of some pet dog—"

"What's wrong? You don't like dogs?"

"I guess I do, after a fashion."

Burcell's eyes narrowed when Dynasty smiled and made a slight hand gesture. To give him credit, he stiffened and glanced around him, bracing himself for something. Lupe was coming up on his blind side, though. "Meet Lupe," Dynasty went on. "You could call her a dog. Our vet thinks she's mostly arctic wolf. We like to think she's a native New Yorker."

Aaron turned in slow motion, catching the gray blur as it went past him to Dynasty. Then it whirled in front of her, facing him, teeth bared. "Lupe," he said, his tone coaxing. "Beautiful." He looked at Dynasty. "It's not illegal in this state to keep wild animals?"

"Perhaps it is. She came to me three years ago, shortly after my arrival, on a winter's night, torn and bleeding. I don't know what she'd tangled with, nor did my vet. When she was washed and medicated she was quiet, mostly sleeping, for almost two days, then pretty down-and-out for the six after that." She patted the head that came above her waist. "By the time she was well enough to move around freely, she called this home. She's used to us. If she's wild, she hasn't told us."

"She's a barrel o' laughs," Dorothy muttered, eyeing the beast. "Putting her in the bathtub wasn't the smartest move—"

"It was before the workers came—"

"A plumber, an electrician, as well as a mason. Humph! Even as weak as she was, she scared the hell out of all of them, not to mention nearly drowning us."

Dynasty frowned at her, then turned back to Aaron Burcell. "Now that you know we don't have your horse, sir, and that I do like canines . . . of a type, I'll say good-bye. I should get back to work—"

"I'd like to see your horses."

"Look, Mr. Burcell, get this straight. What's on this farm is mine. I don't have anyone else's stock." She hauled in an angry breath. "I had no intention of having horses on this farm. A friend took me to a sale in Ithaca. That's in Tompkins County—"

"I know Ithaca. I attended Cornell."

"Whoopee. So did I. I still don't consider you a sorority sister, Mr. Burcell—"

"I'm devastated."

"Thought you might be."

Dorothy snorted. "Never saw such people for going off on side streets. Stick to the topic. You were talking about the horses." She shrugged when Dynasty glowered at her.

Dynasty cleared her throat. "If you know the area, then you should be aware they have a mustang sale every spring. I was dragged to it and convinced I should find a place for the homeless—"

"Laudable. First wolves. Then horses."

"Wolf. Singular." She grabbed her pitchfork, which she'd stabbed into the ground beside her. "I'm busy—"

"No problem. I can look at the horses without you. I noticed them pasturing as I drove in here. I'll just wander over—"

"In those Italian leather shoes? Keep an open mind to sliding on some interesting droppings—"

"I know horses, Ms. Jones . . . and the leftovers."

"Not these. They're mustangs, Mr. Burcell. Wild. They've come to know us after a fashion and accept us in some ways, but they're still skittish . . . Wait! Where are you going?" She jabbed the pitchfork back into the ground, feeling it quiver under her hand. She jogged after him, calling back to Dorothy, "Bring the gun."

"That's a little premature, isn't it? Should I wing him or drill him?"

Dynasty didn't answer her smirk. "Fire into the air if one of those mustangs goes for him. What else can we do?"

"Starting a stampede isn't the best idea you've ever had."

"You can't start one of those with six horses . . . can you?"

Dorothy rolled her eyes. "Why did I get a city slicker?"

Dynasty's smile was acid. "You have to pay for your sins, Dorothy. You talked me into the horses. Hurry. He's liable to get my new fence ripped to pieces."

"We have mustangs, not Clydesdales."

"Thank you for the input," she called over her shoulder, and ran after the interloper. Suits! Was she never going to be free of them? Damn, he was fast. "Stop! If you upset them, Mr. Burcell—" She tripped on one of the many rocks on the property. Down she went, facefirst in the too-long grass. A nice lawn wasn't a high priority. "Damn!" She pushed up to all fours, then felt herself lifted to her feet. "Thanks. I'm fine."

She brushed herself off, then glanced up at him. A

funny, shivery sensation, like walking through a gaggle of mud hornets, assailed her. He had such unusual eyes. Green as emeralds with topaz circling the iris. Eagle eyes. His smile twisted, one eyebrow raising a tad. She'd been staring! "Sorry. Habit. Always study strangers."

"Lived in the big city?"

"For a time." She walked beside him to the high fence. "There." She pointed across the pasture to a cluster of weeping willows whose trunks were so thick, they resembled oaks. They'd wound themselves around one another, so it looked like a wall of trees. Rather than standing a row, they were off centered and provided a massive shade space for the horses. "Mustangs."

Burcell leaned his forearms on the fence. "An assortment from chestnut to gray," he muttered.

"Yes. That's what—Hey! Don't do that. It's dangerous." Openmouthed, she watched him vault over the fence, using his hands and powerful arms as leverage to swing his body over and to the ground.

He turned around and looked at her. "No Gucci slip-ons, Ms. Jones. Don't worry."

Dynasty climbed up and straddled the fence. "Dammit, if you upset them, you'll . . . Oh Lord, you've spooked them." Astounded, she watched the horses turn toward them and begin to trot, then canter, then open to a gallop in their direction.

"Maybe not," he murmured.

The lead horse came straight at Burcell, head out, mane flying, hooves thundering.

"Dorothy! The gun!"

"Do nothing," Burcell bellowed.

Dynasty froze atop the fence. She felt rather than saw Dorothy come to the fence, heard her indrawn breath. "He'll be killed."

"He'd better not sue."

At the last possible moment, Stormy, the biggest and the best of the small herd, veered to the side, then reared.

Burcell held up his arms, palms out, talking in a singsong way.

The horse shook his head as he came down. He tore at the ground with one hoof, eyeing Burcell.

The others thundered up behind Stormy, bumping, circling, stamping. They neighed, tossed their heads, nostrils flaring, hooves coming up high. One or two bared teeth. One had his ears back.

"Oh dear," Dorothy said. "Buster seems a tad upset."

"He'll bite Burcell's nose off, quick as a flash, if he doesn't move."

All at once, Stormy subsided. He snorted, then moved forward. He nuzzled Burcell's chest hard enough to take him to the ground. Burcell slightly staggered, then caught the horse along its strong jaw. "Moonstruck, big guy, how are you?"

"His name is Stormy," Dynasty said. "He's just fine. Now come out of there."

Burcell glanced around, glowering. "Can't you see he knows me? That we have a kinship."

"Of course. He's your uncle Louie. I couldn't

miss the resemblance, especially between you and Stormy's rump."

Dorothy burped, excused herself, and hiccuped.

Silence stretched.

"I'll have a trailer here tomorrow," Burcell said.

"You try taking that horse out of here, and I'll use that gun on you."

"I can show you markings—"

"So can I. That horse has been abused. Both Dorothy and I saw it. We thought it was some disgusting tourist throwing stones and sticks." Forgetting where she was, and her wariness concerning horses, she got down inside the pasture. "You'll not take him from this farm. I'll have you arrested if you try." She walked over to the horse and lifted her hand to his muzzle, rubbing it, cooing to him. "Don't you worry. Your abuser is out of here."

"I . . . don't . . . abuse . . . anything," Burcell said, fury in every line of his face.

She whirled like a spitting tiger. "Then why was he on his way to a dog food factory? If I hadn't adopted him he'd be kibble by now, Mr. Burcell. Got that?"

"I did. So did everyone for miles around, Ms. Jones. You bent those trees, lady."

With her back to the stallion, she opened her mouth to tear a strip off the stranger.

Stormy chose that moment to be playful. He butted her in the back, hard, catapulting her against Aaron Burcell's chest.

Burcell's musky male scent came through the

super soft cotton of his shirt, wafting around her like a hypnotic draft. She inhaled even as her inner self told her to smack him. To move back, take charge. She lifted her head with an effort. The green eyes made her forget the scathing comment that'd trembled on her tongue. "Ah . . . Mr. Burcell . . . Leave."

"With the horse," he said, his tone whisper-soft, his arms still around her.

"No," she muttered. "I'll get my lawyer." Would she have to go as far as the county seat for one? She'd never seen a shingle when she'd gone into Remus, the nearest town. Could she even afford one? She'd scrounge the money somewhere.

"Why? I can prove he's mine."

"And I can prove he's been abused. And I have the papers describing him and calling him mine." With every ounce of strength she possessed she brought her hands up between them and pushed. "Our veterinarian has the records. I have the copies." Years of keeping close, tight books stood her in good stead in this instance.

Burcell let her go so suddenly, she almost fell to the ground. "I didn't do it. I don't hurt animals."

She inhaled, feeling giddy. He had the most piercing eyes. "I don't know you well enough to take your word."

"I'll get people who will swear to my veracity and my good treatment of animals . . . and people."

Dynasty stiffened. What did he mean? She wished she were a better judge of character. It might have saved her grief on the Street. "I won't let Stormy go. He's mine."

Burcell swallowed. "How much do you know about thoroughbreds? About flat racing?"

"Next to nothing."

"Then why do you want to keep him?"

"I like to ride him."

Burcell's mouth dropped. "You . . . ride a thoroughbred?"

"Why not? I had to learn on something. And he likes the exercise."

"You learned on him?"

"Yes. Your voice is very hoarse. You might be coming down with something. Or, worse, you could be allergic. It's the grasses. You'd better leave Yokapa County. We have rabies here."

"Do you intend to bite me?"

Anger swelled in her. "I'm not letting him go, Aaron Burcell. He likes me to ride him . . . and I'm good to him." She took a deep breath. "We're friends."

"He's extremely valuable now, and will be even more so when he's put to stud."

"Just a jock like you, huh?"

Dorothy coughed.

Burcell inclined his head. "Why, Ms. Jones, are you testing me?"

"Bug off."

The smile lingered in his eyes, though his words were serious. "I wasn't kidding about his worth. People have killed horses like him to collect on insurance." He held up one hand. "No. I wouldn't do that, either."

"Somebody sure tried to finish him." She lifted her chin. "He had welts an inch high all over his back, chest, and legs. He was beaten," she said through her teeth.

"I'll buy him."

"The money doesn't interest me." She saw his glance flick from the rusted barn to the paint peeling on the house. "No matter the price."

"As I said he's worth millions."

"Would you pay that?"

"Almost."

"Then you'd better know something. He's worth millions to me as my friend."

Burcell stared at her for long seconds, a muscle jumping in his cheek. "It's a stupid move . . . and it could be dangerous."

"I've been called stupid before, Burcell. And I've been threatened too."

"I didn't call you that. Nor would I threaten you. I said it was a stupid move. It is. I said it could be dangerous. It could." He swung on his heel, striding to the fence, then vaulted back over it. "I'll return."

"Be still my heart."

"I heard that," he said over his shoulder.

"Save yourself a trip." Dynasty followed to the fence, leaning against it, all but ignoring the tons of unpredictable equines behind her. Stormy nuzzled her. She stared at Aaron Burcell, reaching up to pat the horse. "Don't worry. You're staying with me, big guy. Nobody's going to push me around, ever again. They're not getting you, either."

He butted her once more, then turned and trotted back across the pasture to the shady copse. The others hesitated, then followed him.

Dorothy moved to the fence. "Made a big impression on Aaron Burcell. He'll probably ask you for a date."

"Dating's not in vogue anymore." Dynasty watched him as he passed the barn. He had a long stride . . . and legs.

"In or out, he won't be calling you." Dorothy screwed up her face. "Never knew anybody who could sink her boat faster'n you."

"It's in my gene pool."

"Bull pucky."

Both women watched the Porsche wend its way down the drive, avoiding most of the ruts.

"Shame about his oil pan," Dorothy said.

"He'll send a bill. Don't worry."

"Maybe he won't."

"I don't need his type."

"Not every thousand-dollar Suit is a crook."

Dynasty glared at Dorothy, then climbed the fence and dropped to the ground next to her. "How do you know? I met a gaggle of them on the Street, and it wasn't a fun time. When the chips are down, the only thing first class about men like that is the fabric on their backs and the leather briefcases they carry."

Dorothy shook her head. "Not all of them."

"Enough." She'd told Dorothy why she'd run from Wall Street, the big city, and a six-figure salary. After five successful years as a stockbroker, she'd been stunned to learn she was being charged with illegal trading of junk bonds. She was sure she'd been set up to take the fall for someone else, but whoever that person was, he covered his tracks too well. "Most of my coworkers knew I was honest, that I hadn't been involved in any shady trading, even though, as it turned out, some in our firm were. Not one of my colleagues came forward to testify for me, though."

"This one has a good look about him," Dorothy said, "and not just because he's taller than my Ned, who was six feet two in his socks." Dorothy looked thoughtful. "Ned didn't have that glossy chestnut hair just like one of those geldings yonder." Dorothy tilted her head. "I'll bet he looks good stripped down too. Good legs. Nice hips. And he's got a butt to cry for—"

"Dorothy!"

"A woman looks, too, you know. I'm middle-aged, not Jurassic period." She pursed her lips. "I'll bet he's the one who rented Junior Blessing's place."

"That stone pile? No one's been in it for years, you said."

Dorothy nodded. "Junior hates Yokapa County. Stays in those condos he built in Florida most of the time. When he comes up here, he stays in the town houses to the north of us, along the lake. To give the devil his due, they're not half bad. Surprised everyone in this county by being smarter than he ever acted around here." She laughed. "Thinks this county's too slow, probably. Fast-track boy is our Junior. Funny thing. When I taught him in grade school he was the one who was slow. How things change."

Dynasty laughed along with Dorothy, but her thoughts weren't on Junior Blessing. They were on Aaron Burcell. Who was he? Besides being a horseman, there were unplumbed depths to him. She'd seen it in his eyes. It upset her to have him stay on her mind. With most men, clearing them out of her brain was easy. The steel gate she'd kept around her being had creaked open. She didn't like it. She'd promised herself she'd never trust the Suits again. She wouldn't. No matter what Dorothy thought he was, to her he was the enemy.

TWO

"Dex? It's Aaron. Thanks for the tip. The house is great." Aaron cradled the phone against his shoulder. "I'm thinking of a long-term lease."

"Why, for God's sake?" his friend asked. "You're in the midsection of New York State. The coast is where the action is, friend. Nothing happens in Yokapa County. I mean, you can stand at a fence and count cows. Nothing else. What'll you do for fun?"

"Not much." Aaron chuckled. There was always Dynasty Jones. Maybe over dinner they could discuss Moonstruck. She was so damned quick off the mark . . .

"Are you listening to me, Aar?"

"Yes. You think I've lost my mind because I want to lease near Honeysuckle Farm."

"Is that where the horse is? Cute name."

"I'm pretty sure it's Moonstruck. I'll bring in Rory to check him over and see if any of the markings have been removed. To answer your question, why the lease, I need a place that I can come to in a hurry. There's too much doing in Kentucky to allow for lengthy visits here. I intend to stay as close as possible on this. I'll need all the information I can gather here." And Dynasty Jones was just the person to give it to him. Unless she lost her temper and told him to get lost. She was beautiful. More spirited than Kiltie Dea's mare, Starlight. What would Dynasty Jones do if she knew he'd compared her to a horse? He chuckled.

"What? What are you laughing about, Aar?"

"Inside joke." Dexter Beaman hadn't changed since they'd been roommates their freshman year at Cornell. Even after Aaron had switched to Harvard, they'd remained fast friends. In later years Dex had become Aaron's stockbroker, and they'd often vacationed together. Whenever Aaron was in New York, they met for dinner. Dex was a good man . . . and he was addicted to gossip. Aaron wasn't going to discuss Dynasty Jones with him.

"Thirdhand information does pay off, right, Aar? When will you be able to get the horse to Kentucky?"

"I'm not sure. Even after I confirm it's him, he'll need a thorough going-over by a good vet before I'd risk trailering him."

"Right."

Aaron exhaled. "I think I owe you big on this one, Dex."

"It's great to think you found him."

"He's got some healed lesions on his coat, some serious ones. He's thinner, but I knew him and he knew me. Since he's been at Honeysuckle Farm, he's had good care, from what I could tell. He looks like he could recover." Aaron cursed. "I'd like to find the person who worked him over."

"Damn! It's incredible. I thought it was a shot in the dark at best." Dex paused. "Poor Casey. I'll bet he died trying to save that horse. How Moonstruck ended up herded with mustangs, and not slaughtered like so many of them, will probably remain a mystery."

"Not if I can help it."

"Aar, I don't think you have a prayer of solving this. Inside information says the abduction and slaughter of high-priced thoroughbreds is high on the power curve. Big dollars and a big, extensive operation. I've asked a few questions since this came up."

"Casey was one of the best trainers we had. And a damned good friend. That's why he ran the stud farm. And why his son Rory is in charge now. Casey was like a second father to me. My family won't rest until we find out who killed him, and who stole Moonstruck."

"The people who did it were smart, Aaron. They knew exactly how to pull it off with little fuss. Casey must've surprised them. Not too many horse trainers are as conscientious as he was. He spent more time in the barn than he did anywhere else." Dex paused. "They must've hit when Casey was alone, or maybe when he was asleep. I don't think you'll ever solve this. If you do, I want to be the first to know."

Aaron was silent for a moment. "Casey might've suspected something like this because of Andromeda. I guess we got careless. Losing a great horse like Andromeda should've put us on guard. We were fools to think we wouldn't get hit twice in a short time."

Dex sighed. "What can I say? This manner of stealing has erupted in most businesses. Look at mine. Wall Street was awash with wealthy thieves a few years back. Sure, some of them went to jail. Few of them lost the funds they stole, though. After they do their time in some fancy hotel atmosphere, they come out rich men. Who can explain it? Back to your problem. Tell me about Dynasty Jones."

"She's one tough young lady."

"Oh? Interesting."

"She doesn't want to give up the stallion. Says she rides him every day—"

"What? Did I hear you right? A multimillion-dollar racehorse who's won some very prestigious races for two-year-olds, not to mention what his worth will be as a stud . . . and she rides him for recreation every day?"

"Yes."

"I can recommend a psychiatrist."

"Insane doesn't fit. Fey could describe her better." Aaron recalled her creamy skin, the red hair strapped back into a tight ponytail. If there'd been anything on that delicate skin but sunblock, he hadn't seen it. There'd been fire in those flashing violet eyes, temper in the angle of her tilted chin. Plain gorgeous. Getting to know her could be more than interesting. "She's . . . unusual."

"Intriguing. I might pay my alma mater a visit—"

"No need." Aaron hesitated. "You might ask your other former classmate what he wants to lease his place, six months or more."

"What? That long? Dynasty Jones must be outstanding."

"She told me to get the hell off her property."

"More and more interesting."

"I have to go, Dex, I'm—"

"Just be careful. The Boehrman-Dearman incident that she was involved in was bad. Cal Steelman, who was on the board, gave me my information. A hell of a thing." Long pause. "Most of the dealers who were charged managed to squeak out from under by rolling over for the feds. Not Dynasty Jones. They never found the shares that disappeared. No doubt everything got washed through the Grand Caymans." Dex cleared his throat. "I thought she got shafted. There are some on the Street who still say she was dirty."

Anger coursed through Aaron. He bit back a retort, knowing he couldn't and wouldn't explain. "She was exonerated. Slate wiped clean, as I understand it."

"Right."

Aaron pictured the fiery redhead who'd confronted him, her eyes stormy and defiant. Even if she'd been a crook, he wouldn't have passed up the chance to meet her.

He remembered a news clip of her entering the courthouse back when she was on trial. She'd been a soignée redhead, slim as a reed, dressed to the nines, striding beside her voluble lawyer, everything seeming in place. Even on impersonal television, she'd arrested his attention. The Dynasty Jones he'd just met had traded in the sophistication for scruffy sneakers and soft, well-worn jeans. The woman on television had had no hair out of place, but the Dynasty Jones of Honeysuckle Farm had curls sticking to her neck and forehead in the damp heat.

Dex's voice interrupted Aaron's musings. "Have you considered, Aaron, that she might be part of the scheme to steal Moonstruck?"

Aaron pictured her with Moonstruck, cooing to the big horse, patting his snout. She hadn't been totally at ease with the horse, but she'd tried to comfort it. "She doesn't fit the picture of someone who'd slaughter a thoroughbred for insurance, or trade it off to a low-grade stud farm."

"Impressed you, did she?"

"Yes." He was more than impressed. He was knock-down, drag-out intrigued. That hadn't happened in a long time.

"I'd like to meet the lady," Dex said.

"If I need you, I'll call. Get in touch with my landlord. That's how you can help me. I'd like to settle on a lease."

"Right."

THREE

The morning beamed with burning sun, blue sky, and a fluffy skirt of cirrus clouds as Dynasty walked out to the stables. A hand-laundered day is how Dorothy would describe it. Dynasty inhaled the freshness and agreed. Everything was vivid. Emerald-green grass and trees with branches turned black from morning dew, complemented the azure heavens slashed with white. An earthy primitive landscape done in three dimension.

The big sliding door on the short side of the rectangular barn was latched within to a support beam. In the middle of the sliding door was a smaller door. She unhooked it and entered the dark interior, feeling along until she found the latch and released it. Sliding the door back, baring the wide area in front of the stalls to the sun and the morning freshness, she smiled when she heard the soft whinnies. She put some mash in the bags, inhaling the sweet, pungent odor of clean hay. Her nose twitched, catching the acrid lacing of manure.

"Hi, guys. I'm here." After releasing five of the horses into the pasture, she went back to Stormy, talking to him while she fitted the tack to him. She was building a rapport with him, even if she did have some uneasy moments. "I'll bet you just tolerate me because I hold the feed bag strings. Maybe the gleam in those big brown eyes means you'll take a chunk out of me, if I'm not wary." Holding the reins, she led him out of the barn. "You know, Stormy, it surprised me when Dorothy told me horses bite. I knew dogs did . . . and lions and tigers. Somehow it doesn't fit horses. You guys are overwhelming because of size, not incisors. Right? I'd better get another book from the library about your kind."

Stormy snorted. Dynasty stepped back, then moved closer. "Yes, yes, I know. I should be used to your games by now. Look at it from my point of view. You've only been here six weeks. We're not bosom buddies." She stroked his velvety nose. "I haven't been around that many horses, you know. Even with Dorothy's tutoring and those pamphlets from the Cooperative Extension, I'm not oozing knowledge or confidence." She moved her hand up and down the muzzle. "You're so lovely, though. Would you like to go for a little ride? Maybe down to the beach?" When he nickered again, she laughed. Not since she'd left New York three years ago had she felt such warmth. Almost, the ice in her soul cracked. Maybe in time it would melt.

She adjusted the tack on the horse, wondering for the hundredth time why it took her twice as long as it took Dorothy who seemed to throw everything at the horse and have it all in place in a flash.

She cinched the saddle, checking it twice as she'd been shown. "Now, remember, your job is to remain still. Then I get on . . . no, mount. Okay? Great. Here I go." Dynasty bit her bottom lip, grasped the reins, then the pommel. Left foot in the stirrup. Taking a deep breath, she heaved up and over, rocking, gripping the reins too hard. When he jerked his head back, she released the death hold.

"Good boy. You know how stupid I am and have decided to be patient," she muttered, patting the glossy neck. She exhaled. He was certainly high. Tapping the shiny chestnut sides with her heels, she gulped at the instant motion. "Whoa. Easy now."

He moved as smooth as maple syrup. Or like a Porsche. No! Don't think about Aaron Burcell, she told herself. He'd taken up too much of her sleep time last night. No wonder she had enough luggage under her eyes for a world tour. Get lost, Burcell. She wouldn't spend one more second thinking about his green eyes, wide shoulders, smooth gait, and corkscrew smile. They had no importance in her life.

As though Stormy sensed her need to go slowly, the horse broke to a walk.

"Better." Dynasty lifted her hands as Dorothy'd taught her, feeling the animal respond. Turning the chestnut, she angled him down past the house to the lower pasture that led for half a mile to the high plateau overlooking beautiful Cayuga Lake. Once before she'd taken Stormy to the beach, letting him cool off in the shiny clean water. Dorothy had told her that others along the beach actually swam with their horses. Dynasty took that with a grain of salt. She just couldn't imagine it. "Today, I'll swim. You wade, Stormy."

Swimming had been her solace in Manhattan. It had helped with the initial loneliness when the world had broken up around her. Now it was pure recreation. She had no need to burn up the calories to blot out the mind. Swimming was for leisure . . . unless Aaron Burcell took too many places in her thoughts. Then she'd start the punishing workouts that had left her breathless.

Brushing away her old life hadn't been easy. Some particles still clung to her, such as an eagerness to do well in the market. This time with berries, not bonds. She patted the long neck in front of her. "I guess we could speed it up a little, big guy."

She allowed her body to go with the animal in the "posting" rhythm demanded for easy riding. Looking out over the lake ahead of her, she sighed. The serene beauty of her surroundings was her bulwark.

She liked her solitary life and wanted no other.

So why had Aaron Burcell burst in on it? She wouldn't let him bring back the chaos. Yet his handsome face and rugged body had walked through her head all night. He had wonderful hands, well-kept long fingers. What would it be like to be held again by him? She hadn't been able to blot from her mind the memory of when he'd lifted her and suspended her in his hold.

Aaron Burcell's appearance had sharpened memories she wanted to bury. David Lear had been tall, like Aaron Burcell. He'd told her he loved her. When she'd been charged, he'd faded from her life. Before her trial ended he'd become engaged to a neophyte broker named Jennifer. It hadn't been the loss of a love that had hurt. She had realized that she hadn't loved David any more than he'd loved her. It'd been the loss of faith, the absence of trust. She should've been able to expect a measure of confidence, a belief in her honesty, from a friend and lover. It had been gall, a bitter swallowing that had almost choked her.

David hadn't been the only one. Few of her associates on Wall Street had come forward to support her. Sometimes she thought she really couldn't blame them. More than once during the long ordeal of the trial, she'd begun to wonder herself if she was guilty. She'd been so alone, cut off. Every day there seemed to be more and more rumors about her veracity and integrity. In her heart she'd known her culpability had been in trusting the wrong people.

Not that she hadn't known about Wall Street thievery, about the high-tech robbers who'd become billionaires on the backs of hapless investors. Until she'd been subpoenaed she hadn't realized it was in her own backyard, and that a hill of evidence pointed to her. Thank heavens her attorney hadn't backed down. Dee Brown had come out swinging, gunning for the right verdict. They'd won against an ava-

lanche of trumped-up charges and damning eviden-
tiary material that had made her quail, more than
once. They'd won against great odds.

Shaking her head, Dynasty kneed the mount,
urging it to a canter. Focused on keeping her seat,
she all but wiped her mind clean of the past. She was
grateful and kept her eyes on the horse's mane, her
mind on his rhythm.

She reined in at the top of the escarpment, a hundred feet and more above the deserted beach. Five
hundred feet of the beautiful, almost untouched
lakefront belonged to Honeysuckle Farm. Her grandmother had left her a gold mine in frontage alone. To
the north was Junior Blessing's holding, almost a mile
of beach, rarely used by him. To the south were a
series of summer homes all on the escarpment, steep
stairs climbing in zigzag patterns from the docks and
beach area to the plateau.

Dynasty had a road of sorts leading down to hers.
Dorothy had told her that the dock had once been
sturdy. Now it tottered with every wavelet. The
frontage was overgrown with weeds and rocks, but
the water was clear and swimmable. She took a deep
breath as she looked down the narrow passage that
S-curved to the beach. It wasn't much and it needed
work. She'd been assured by Jacob Meistersaenger,
one of her Amish neighbors, that it could be widened
and graded for a car if she wished to tote a boat to the
water and launch it. Since she didn't own a boat, and
doubted one could be tied to the rickety dock, she'd
smiled and said she'd think about it.

"Enough of pondering. Down we go, Stormy," she murmured to the horse.

Going down was a lot tougher than climbing up. On the way down, she couldn't seem to stop sliding toward the horse's neck, no matter how far she leaned back and clutched the horse's flanks with her knees. Why Stormy didn't balk at such steepness, she couldn't figure. He seemed to handle it with ease. She gasped when he jumped the last few feet to the beach and promptly walked into the water.

Dynasty laughed, relieved to be on flat ground. "You're so patient," she told Stormy. "All this time I thought thoroughbreds were temperamental. You're a pussy cat. You deserve to soak your feet . . . er, hooves." She chuckled again, patting Stormy's neck, then angled him back to shore. She dismounted and grinned at the horse. "Stormy, I think we're a couple of misfits. I don't belong on a farm, and you shouldn't be with mustangs." She rubbed her backside. "I've gotten so I hate cowboy movies. They make it look so easy . . . riding a horse, that is. Here, let me loosen this." She lifted the reins over his head, letting them droop. A no-no according to Dorothy. To Dynasty it gave Stormy breathing room. "Be good and don't tell on me. I'll catch hell from Dorothy if you take off."

Stormy nickered, then bumped her shoulder with his nose.

"Oh, no. Not yet. I have treats for you, but first I'm going to swim. Then we'll negotiate." She wore her bathing suit under her clothes. After stripping off her jeans and shirt, she draped them over some tree limbs, then eyed the solitary beach with pleasure. A beautiful curve of stones and sand, weeping willow fronds fanning the air, waterweeds soughing in the breeze like children humming. It was quiet, private. She loved it. The neighbors to the south were only there on weekends. For a mile each way, there was solitary wonder.

She inhaled a deep breath, looking up at the clouds that had formed themselves into communities of puffy white. Soon thunderheads would build. "I will be happy," she told the world above her. "Yesterdays don't count." She looped Stormy's reins over a tree branch near her jeans. "There. Now you have shade, and can get into the water too. Be good. Stay cool. I'll be right back."

She fitted ear plugs, nylon cap, and goggles to her head, then stepped into the water that seemed chilly against her overheated skin. Plunging forward in a shallow dive, she gasped, reveling in the silkiness against her skin. She stroked hard as she always did, her days as a competitor in high school and college coming back to her each time she was in the water. Maybe it wasn't the safest habit, swimming alone. She knew that from working as a lifeguard in college. It still gave her great serenity to be alone and work out in the lake water she loved.

She didn't know how long she swam. When she stopped to float on her back, the clouds were already forming into low-hung thunderheads. They could become balloonish high-rises by afternoon. She had time. She closed her eyes, letting the water soothe her.

The roar of a powerboat suddenly shattered her peace. Eyes fluttering open, then snapping wide as the boat neared, she flipped, taking a mouthful of water. Coughing, blinking, she saw someone throw a box off the stern. Damned polluter! Take your garbage home! The heavy waves struck her face, choking off her protesting cries. Treading water, she watched the craft speed out of sight. To her surprise the box hadn't sunk. Stroking hard, she swam toward it. Maybe she could get it out of the water before it sank and despoiled the lake. Damn the idiots who thought it was okay to dump their refuse in the lake. Breaking the law. If only she'd gotten the number of the boat.

The box nudged against her. She grabbed it, then she heard it. *Meow! Meow!* What on earth . . . ?

The box was getting soggy, heavy. Shifting to her back, she propped it on her middle and kicked hard, glancing toward shore to get her bearings.

Gauging the water's depth by her distance from shore, she soon dropped one foot and found bottom. Gripping the box with two hands, she plowed her way out of the water and set the box down on shore.

Stormy nickered and moved closer. *Meow! Meow!* Cats? They threw cats from the boat? Gagging at the thought of what would've happened had she not been in the water, she pulled at the cardboard top, interwoven to keep it shut. Lifting the flap, she peeked in. "Three. Lord, you're just babies. What am I going to do with you? I don't like cats."

"Stay there," she ordered the felines. She refastened the top, then went to the saddlebags, clucking to Stormy. She had some kibble in the bottom that she kept for Lupe when the wolf accompanied her. It would be too big for the cats to eat. Gripping her water bottle, she went back to the box and opened it. The slightly sodden trio gazed up at her. "Like a drink?" She poured some. They mewed louder. "Oh, dear. You need milk. We'd better get you to the house."

Stormy nickered, louder this time, pulling against his tether.

"We're going back, Stormy. Be patient," Dynasty muttered.

"Now, you're stealing kittens?"

Dynasty's head spun so fast, her neck hurt. Aaron Burcell, looking magnificent atop a beautiful bay horse, was only a few feet away. "You? What're you doing here? This is a private beach. It belongs to Honeysuckle Farm."

"I thought the water's edge belonged to the walker . . . or rider, as the case may be."

Unsure, wary, she stared at him. "You're not at water's edge. Neither is your horse." Her chin went up a notch. "So get on your way . . . off my land."

He leaned over the pommel of the soft western saddle. "And the box with all the meowing. How do you explain that?"

Her chin went up another two notches. "I have no need to explain anything to you." His sudden smile was like a punch in the gut that left her gasping. Charmer!

"Tough, aren't you?"

"Tough enough."

He relaxed, his eyes not leaving hers. "You've proved it against a very tough crowd."

She fought all of it. The blood filling her, staining her face, the weakness in her knees, the boom-boom-ing of her pulse. "So you've heard of me."

He nodded.

"Then guard your wallet, Mr. Burcell. Some would say I'm a dangerous thief."

"I can see that." He jerked his head at the box. "How much do you think they're worth?"

"Huh?" She tore her gaze from his to look at the kittens. "Oh. Them? About . . . about a dollar." She felt dizzy. He had a bad effect on her. If he kept pitching curves, she was bound to get beaned.

"You're overstating. I'd say not more than a nickel for the lot."

"Is that so? These cats could be worth a great deal. For all you know they could be refugee Himalayans." That was one breed name she knew. She bit her lip as the mewling grew louder. "I have to go," she muttered in Aaron Burcell's direction.

"Let me give you a hand." He swung off his horse.

"Where did you get the horse?"

"Belongs to Junior. Here." He pulled a flask from the saddlebag.

"Don't you dare give them alcohol. It would kill

them," she told him as she grabbed his arm and bore down with all her strength.

He lifted his hand, bringing her with it. "Skim milk. I drink it."

Her eyes narrowed. "You do?" Suspicion flooded her. "Let me smell." When he chuckled, she shivered.

"Hey! You're cold." He whipped off his T-shirt and pulled it over her head in one quick jerk, trapping her arms at her sides.

He laughed down at her. "Now I have you where I want you."

She looked at his bared chest. Her mouth went dry. The arrow of hair that veed down to his pull-on cotton pants hypnotized her. "Thanks," she managed to say, "but there's no need. I have clothes."

He pulled the shirt down again when she would've shrugged out of it. "I was too warm anyway. Keep it on, Dynasty Jones."

She was too quivery to do anything, so she nodded.

"Now, should we give them milk?"

She bobbed her head up and down again.

Together they watched the little things drink milk from leaves they bent in the shape of cups.

Dynasty was flustered, but the thought that had intruded in some of her sleeplessness the previous night surfaced. "Who told you I had Stormy?"

"A friend of my stockbroker."

She stiffened. "I see."

"No, you don't. It had nothing to do with you

being accused, then exonerated, of a crime. It had to do with some heavy investigating by people trained to pick up on any rumor that might lead them to horse thieves. The Ithaca roundup was mentioned because someone, I don't know who, had heard about a thoroughbred being hidden in a herd of workhorses that were then tracked to Mexico. A connection was made. We were informed. I arrived."

"That simple?"

"Yes."

Dynasty looked away from him, out over the lake.

"Water nice?" he asked somewhere not far above her ear.

"Yes." Breathing shouldn't be so difficult. It was like being in the middle of a smoke bomb. Maybe he was for real. Dorothy could be right. Not all Suits were crooks.

"Do you sail?"

"Never have. I knew you did."

"How?"

"The way you dress."

"The Italian leather thing?"

"Something like that." So damned inane, she thought. What were they talking about? "I should go."

"I'll go with you." At her narrowed stare, he shrugged. "You could drop the box."

"Oh."

"Are you warming up? Maybe you'd like to swim."

"I did that. You do it. I'll take care of the kittens."

"Your graciousness unmans me."

Dynasty turned. "You're so full of yourself, it'd take a sixteen-wheeler to do that." When he laughed, she was caught in a quivering aura. It took all her self-will to recall how trusting she'd been before, and how it had almost cost her her freedom. Over and over she reminded herself to be very wary. "I'm not impressed."

"Golly, I thought you were."

His soft, satirical tone was like sandpaper to her nerves. "Go away."

"No. I'd better help. You wouldn't want me to return all my merit badges, would you?"

Stony-faced, she gathered up her things, refastened the box, handed him his shirt, tugged her jeans up her legs, yanked on the tank top, and slipped wet feet into her sneaks. Then she went to the horse. "Stormy, if you love your oats, don't sidle," she said between her teeth.

The horse nickered and stood still.

In the saddle Dynasty wanted to kiss the big horse. "Good day," she said to Burcell.

"I'm following you back to your house."

"You look hot. The water's fine. You should swim."

"I am hot, but I'll wait."

The words shivered up and down her spine. She wouldn't look at him, or question if his comment had a double meaning. Maybe she could pretend he wasn't behind her.

"Ms. Jones, you have a great . . . seat."

She swallowed ire, embarrassment, and the urge to gallop. Worse, she wanted to laugh.

"For an animal lover—" he went on.

"I'm not," she said, so fierce, she almost lost her hold on the box. "Easy, Stormy. It's very steep."

"All right. For an animal hater—"

"I do not hate animals." At her raised voice, Stormy hunched forward in giant steps. "Whoa," Dynasty squealed.

"What did you say?"

She took time to adjust to the gait of the horse, loop her hands in the reins, before shooting a glance behind her. "Not that it's any of your business, Adam Burcell, but I give to Greenpeace and to the preservation of the spotted owl. I—I just don't need animals in my life."

"Ah. That's why you keep a wolf, mustangs, a thoroughbred . . . and soon to be cats. Just a show of force in case Wall Street decides to counter attack?"

"You're an idiot," Dynasty said through her teeth. She shoved down hard on the errant amusement bubbling inside her. There was nothing amusing about what she'd gone through . . . yet, she couldn't deny the mirth. Maybe she was beginning to shelf some of her resentment. Forget the introspection, she told herself. Much good it did. Concentrate on getting up the hill with the box of cats.

She reached the plateau, sweating and red-faced. She couldn't indulge in a trot much less a canter. To her chagrin, Aaron Burcell edged his horse next to her.

"Want me to carry the box for a while?" he asked.

In a flash she handed the box to him. Then she kneed Stormy into a canter. She was bounced around more than she liked, but she didn't mind. Besides, in some ways, she could look on it as a lesson in riding. She'd leave him in the dust, even if she would have a sore backside. He was far behind her. . . . In her peripheral vision she caught the motion of his horse next to her. For a second she closed her eyes, not believing he could be there. Then she opened them as quick, for fear of losing her balance.

"Great day for a ride, isn't it, Ms. Jones?"

"You bet," she grated.

"Dorothy told me the two of you would be going to the dance at the gun club tonight."

"They might not let me in. I'm against guns."

"Tough position to be in around here, I'd say."

"I don't preach. I just don't allow them on my land."

"Principle."

"You don't believe in it?"

"I didn't say that."

They were approaching the fenced area of the middle pasture. The house was just on the next knoll. "I can take it from here. Thank you."

"It's fine. Don't fall off your horse. I told Dorothy I'd pick both of you up for the dance since your truck is acting up."

"What?" She rocked in the saddle. "Don't

bother. It stalls now and then. Not a problem. I can drive."

"So can I."

"We won't fit in your Porsche."

"I have another vehicle."

"Gosh, how great."

"Mustn't be sour, Ms. Jones."

"Ordinarily I'm not."

"So you'll go with Dorothy and me?"

Dynasty inhaled. "Guess so."

"You'll never know how happy that makes me."

"We live to please you," she muttered.

"I heard that," he said. "I'll be back with a truck as soon as I've settled you with your brood." At her questioning look, he grinned. "To take your new arrivals to the vet. They'll need checking."

They crossed the middle pasture, going through the wide corral to the opening on the far side that led to the yard and the barn.

Dynasty stared at Stormy's mane. Another vet bill. Lord! More money. "You don't have to bother returning. I can—"

"I know. I'll be back."

"Right." She took the box and watched him canter across the field. He and the horse looked mortared to each other. "Show off," she said, relieved that her pulse had stopped racing.

At the stable she dismounted, or more to the point, she fumbled and slid off. Falling to the ground, the box cuddled to her, she reopened the top. A shadow crossed in front of her. She looked up, shielding her eyes from the glare of morning sun.

"What've you got there?"

"Ah, hello, Merry. Done for the day?"

"Yep." She swiped at her forehead. "Though I think I can use more money for the work I do."

"You've only been here an hour, at most."

Merry's mouth tightened. "I do a lot when I'm here."

"What might that be? Changing the channel to watch three soaps simultaneously?"

Affronted, Merry pursed her lips, then gazed down into the box. "Oooo, cats. Hate 'em. They're dirtier'n dogs. Don't bring 'em in the house."

Swelling with an indignation that encompassed Merry's summary dismissal of the kittens, Aaron Burcell's appearance on her horizon, and the deep-seated worry that they wouldn't have as many gooseberries to harvest as they should, Dynasty scrambled to her feet, cradling the box. She cleared her throat, staring at Merrybelle Betterbole. "I'll pay you for today and yesterday. That makes us even. I'll call you when . . . if I need you again."

Merry's mouth dropped open. "What? I have a job here. Three days a week. What will you do without me?"

"Stumble along. See Dorothy. Tell her what I said. She'll pay you."

Merry flounced around, muttering to herself, and stomped back to the kitchen.

The next thing Dynasty heard was Dorothy's booming laughter.

Dynasty removed Stormy's saddle, wiped him down, and released him into the pasture with the other horses.

Merry was starting up her rattly car with the muffler missing just as Dynasty finished with the horse. Aaron Burcell was coming down the driveway in a four-by-four pickup truck.

"Yoo-hoo. Aaron Burcell," Merry called out her open window. "You should come to our house to dinner one night."

"Thank you, Merrybelle. I wish I had more time to socialize. I don't." Burcell waved, not pausing as he steered around her, and parked not far from Dynasty. "Let's go."

Dynasty nodded, annoyed at his peremptory manner, though she was sure she should get to the vet as soon as possible. Did cats get pneumonia if they got wet? If the kittens had as many fleas as Lupe had had at first, it wouldn't be a good plan to take them into the house before they were treated, even if they were well. "I have to tell Dorothy where I'm going, and get some milk," she said over the roar of Merry's car as it spun down the rutted driveway.

"Tell me what?" Dorothy asked, appearing around the corner of the house. "I see you got some sense, firing that—Good Lord! Where'd you find them? Someone drop them from a car?"

"Worse," Dynasty replied, moving to the passenger side of Burcell's truck. "They dropped them from the back of a boat."

Dorothy shook her head. "Are we turning this into a rescue center for assorted critters?"

"Here. Hold them. I have to get milk." Dynasty jogged to the house, ignoring Aaron Burcell's laughter.

FOUR

"Hickory, Dickery, and Doc? That's what she calls them?"

Dorothy nodded. "Two females, and Doc, the male. All wormed and full o' shots. That set her back a peg." Dorothy looked at her watch. "She's late. They'll be dancing before we get there."

"We'll make up for it." Aaron had wondered all day if Dynasty would back out of going with him and Dorothy to the dance.

"She'll be right along," Dorothy assured him.

"You said something about the cats and vet bill."

Dorothy pursed her lips. "She isn't made of money, you know."

Her worried frown allowed him the question. "Is the farm her only income?"

Dorothy shook her head. "It's mostly her savings, the berries, and her job that support this place. Her gramma Peabody left it to her, but it's gotten pretty run-down by the time she took it over. There were some outstanding debts, and the taxes are high in Yokapa County. . . ." Dorothy shook her head. "Without the money from those articles, she'd go under, I think. Comes in handy."

"Articles," Aaron prodded, excusing his lack of discretion by assuring himself he had her best interests at heart. That he had profound interest in every aspect of Dynasty Jones from her first breath until he set eyes on her; that he wanted to have an enormous stake in her future, was something he chose to ignore. Since first meeting her, she'd had a profound effect on his digestive system, his breathing, and his ability to calculate every move he made. He'd always had pride in that. She'd blown it to hell. She was driving him nuts! He had her on his mind too much. He should've taken his horse and run. Instead, he felt bound to her. It didn't set well to push her on the ownership of Moonstruck, either.

Dorothy smiled at him. "She's diamond sharp, our Dynasty. Writes a column for the *Wall Street Journal*. Never read it much myself. Now, I read it every day."

Somehow Aaron wasn't surprised, though hearing it rocked him right in the gut. She was brighter than a dime, with a mind that was butcher-knife sharp. And she'd taken more kicks than a stable wall, from people she'd expected to trust. He swallowed a sickening sensation. He'd known what she was at first meeting when those violet eyes had fixed on him. She was incapable of chicanery . . . and he would've bet

Burcell Farms and all of its stock on that . . . She'd referred to him as a horse's ass, and he'd felt like one since she'd first given him that direct stare of hers. Nothing would've convinced him that he could fall in love, let alone at first meeting, especially after her unflattering assessment. He chuckled. Was this the real thing? Maybe it wasn't love. He only knew he'd like to spend about seventy years with her and find out. She was sexy as hell, smart, had too much compassion. The love at first sight thing was a fool's game, and he wasn't that kind of player. Still, something had hit him behind the knees.

"You in a dream world?"

He shook himself and looked at Dorothy.

"Ah. Sorry."

"We were talking about Dynasty and her articles."

"I've never seen her name."

"Sure you have." Dorothy chuckled. "She writes under the name Jones Peabody. Peabody was her grandmother's name. 'Analytical Definitions and Projections.' 'Investing and Protecting Them: A Guide for The Neophyte.' That's two of her big ones. Page one for the second one. I've got them all if you'd like to read some."

"I would. Jones Peabody. That name I've seen." His mind scrambled the factors and pieced together a memory of an insightful, in-depth article he'd read for first-time investors. Clear, to the point, on the money information. She was no lightweight in her field.

Why the pen name? Being D. Jones in the B-D scandal shouldn't close her out from business. She'd been exonerated. If she had the smarts to do in-depth articles for the *Journal*, she had the smarts to compete on the Street. Had it been her choice to leave?

"You hadn't better be thinking bad thoughts about her, Aaron Burcell. She's more honest than a herd of them horse traders down in Kentucky." Dorothy glowered.

Aaron smiled at the belligerence. "I have no doubt of that."

"I won't see her hurt," Dorothy continued, her chin edging up.

"Neither will I."

Abashed, taken aback, she stared at him. "Well I'll be—"

"By the way, Ms. Lesser, have I told you that I think your outfit is very fetching."

"Flatterer. You just want me on your side."

Aaron nodded. "I do." He glanced at his watch. "Is there a reason she isn't ready?"

"She wasn't going to go. I said it would ruin my good time if she didn't."

"Blackmail."

"Yes."

A moment later, Dynasty walked into the living room.

Aaron whistled. "Beautiful." Better than that. She made his mouth go dry, his insides shift, his blood cascade through his veins and arteries. She aroused the hell out of him. At the same time he felt a rush of caring that a fool might call paternal. In the country dance outfit of a flowered skirt that hit just above the knee, an off-the-shoulder cream blouse with the crocheted edgings in blue, sapphire, emerald, and gold, she looked like an angel. Her hair was a bound flame coiled on top of her head, with tendrils drifting about her face. Gypsy earrings of wrought gold rings touched her cheeks, making her eyes glisten purple.

Dorothy nodded. "She cleans up real nice, doesn't she?"

Aaron blinked.

Dynasty burst out laughing.

Aaron was so caught in the musical sound, he felt glued to the floor. "I'll be the most envied man at the dance." To his delight both women blushed.

The long summer twilight had just begun when they went out to the yard.

"Get in first, Dynasty," Dorothy said, gesturing to Aaron's pickup. "I get carsick it I'm not near the window."

"The truck has air-conditioning," Dynasty said. "So it won't make any difference if—"

"Sure it will. If I'm near the window, my mind will tell my innards not to be queasy," Dorothy said. She smiled blandly into Dynasty's disbelieving eyes.

Aaron said nothing. When he climbed in the driver's seat, he took a deep breath. Looking down at Dynasty's knee, inches from his, gave him oxygen problems. Sweat popped out on his upper lip. Swallowing wasn't easy. When he reached to the floor shift, his hand glanced off her. She stiffened. So did he . . . in a very sensitive place. She had more thrust than a rocket. He bit back a groan when she tried to edge away, and her backside brushed his hip. Damned bench seats.

Out the rutted drive to the two-lane highway, past country mailboxes balanced on buckets, poles, fused chains. Some houses were in good shape, some were drooping, others were just hanging on. Some cared, some didn't.

"Take the next right, Aaron," Dorothy said. "Up the hill about a mile. You'll see the sign."

Dorothy seemed to be having a good time. He glanced sideways and caught her grinning. "Ah . . . deserted road."

"That's country," Dorothy said. "My Ned and I used to spark along these roads."

"Spark?" Dynasty said. "I thought you said you weren't from the Jurassic period."

"Sour stomach?" Dorothy inquired.

"You're enjoying this," Dynasty said from the side of her mouth.

"I am," Dorothy said, her voice pitched higher. "Can't remember when I looked forward to a dance more."

Conversation lagged. The hum of the engine, the muted tones of Willie Nelson, and the occasional shifting of the gear were the only sounds.

Aaron felt like he was crazy. Simply being in the truck with Dynasty aroused the hell out of him . . . and they weren't touching, just grazing skin from time to time. She hadn't looked at him once.

"Here's the turn," Dorothy said.

The road dipped, bent, swung through an S-curve lined with swaying trees that were turning black as the light faded.

When they finally wheeled into the well-lit driveway of the Gun Club, the barn doors were wide open, and the sawing of a fiddle was almost as loud as the laughter and greetings.

"Great crowd," Dorothy crowed, throwing open her door and slipping to the ground.

A bear of a man in a plaid cotton shirt and jeans with a crease that could've cut cheese, came up to Dorothy. He swept off his hat and held out his other hand. "Dorothy, I'd like a dance if you've a mind."

"You can, Pepper Lally, if you don't put that fool hat back on. I'd feel like I was under an umbrella."

"Gotta bald spot."

"So? There's no sun to burn it. Lose the hat."

Obediently the man turned and sailed the ten-gallon toward a pickup. It landed in the back. "Now, we can dance."

"First you have to meet someone. You know Dynasty."

"I do. Howdy, ma'am. How're the mustangs doin'?"

"Fine, thank you, Pepper."

Dorothy gestured to Aaron. "Aaron, this is Pepper Lally. He's the farmer who brings our fertilizer and humus. Runs a dairy herd off ninety-six. Has some interesting Clydesdales, Belgians, and other job horses."

"How are you?" Aaron put out his hand. "I'm Aaron Burcell."

"From Kentucky? I heard 'bout ya'. Welcome."

Aaron smiled and nodded, managing not to wince at the man's crushing grip. "Thanks. I'll be in the area for a while. Maybe you'd let me look at your stock."

"You know horses. Wouldn't let you near mine if you didn't. Choose your time. Drop by." Pepper smiled, then glanced at Dorothy, who nodded. "We're going to dance. Don't want to waste the music."

As they followed Pepper and Dorothy, Aaron watched Dynasty from the corner of his eye. He also noted the interested male glances cast her way. "I wish you'd dance with me. Right now. I don't have a death wish, but I'm damned if I'll let any of the locals claim you first." He smiled at her.

"What?" She swallowed. "That's a little caveman for—"

"I know. Italian leather."

"I wasn't going to say that." She bit her lip, a smile edging the corners of her mouth. "Think you could take these country boys?"

"No. But I'll give it my best shot."

Laughter burst from her. "You're either the most cockeyed liar I ever met, or the biggest fool."

Aaron put his arm around her, leading her up the ramp to the cavernous barn, past a disgruntled-looking male whose forearms looked like trees. "You choose. I want to dance."

"I'm not much on country dancing," Dynasty said, watching the swift, sure motions of the couples circling the floor.

"I think it's great. We do this in Kentucky. When we go there you'll enjoy the hoedowns just as much . . . though with a difference." He scooped her into the rhythm and steps, not pausing when she stumbled a couple of times, happy just to be holding her.

"What's . . . what's that? The difference, I mean?" Dynasty asked, a little breathless from the rapid twirling.

"More speed," Aaron whispered. He lifted her and spun her around, laughing when she gasped. She was beautiful. Lithe, athletic, a natural dancer, she'd begun to fit her steps to his as though they'd rehearsed each move. She made him dizzy. A strange sensation. His life had been charted by him; he called the moves. It had all caved in around him from the moment she'd called him a horse's ass.

"What's so funny?" Dynasty asked, looking up at him as they continued to turn around the floor in the slide, pause step of the dance.

"Me."

"I don't understand."

"You're not alone."

Dynasty stopped dead. "What did you mean about going to Kentucky? I'm not going there."

"Sure you are." He pulled her into the dance again, determined to convince her as the idea rooted in his brain and spread through him. "Give me a chance to prove that I wouldn't mistreat Moonstruck and leave him in the condition you found him. Let me prove to you I'm capable of caring for horses and do a good job of it. Only fair, lady. You won't take me on faith—"

"I might. I don't have time to go to Kentucky."

"Sure you do. I'll help you harvest the berries and cart them to New York City—"

"Dorothy and I have managed with some local help."

". . . then, Dorothy can watch the place while you're in Kentucky. I'm sure Pepper Lally will give her a hand."

"He will. He likes her . . . more than a little—"

"There you are. All settled."

"Aaron—"

"I do like the way you say my name." He spun her again, watching the way her skirt frothed around her. She had great legs, and her waist was a perfect fit for his hands. "You have to come to Kentucky. If you don't see the stables for yourself and talk to the people there, you'd never quite trust me . . . even if I just wanted to borrow Moonstruck for stud now and then." When her eyes narrowed, he grinned. "Still suspicious. See? You have to come to Kentucky."

"I'll think about it."

"I'll settle for that." He had no intention of letting her bug out. His pulse rate quickened at the thought of showing her Burcell Farms, the horses, introducing her to his family. She needed to get to know him. Doing just that in Kentucky was a good plan. When her hair tickled his chin as the beat slowed, his heart thumped hard.

Dynasty looked at him. "I've never liked country music that much."

"How about now?"

"It sounds good, I'll admit."

"Would you like a cold drink?" he asked when the music ended.

She nodded, looking around her.

"Do you know everyone?"

"Most everyone. After three years in a small community, you're on speaking terms with those that go to town." She smiled. "Not too many miss market day."

"You're nervous, though." He sensed her reluctance to approach the group at the long table serving refreshments.

She looked surprised. "Maybe."

"Don't be. You're beautiful and kind. That's very special." When she reddened, he wanted to say more.

"Hey, Dynasty. How are you?"

She turned to greet a young man walking toward them.

Aaron grimaced, ordered some drinks, and watched. The close moment they'd almost shared melted away.

FIVE

The harvest was in, boxed, and loaded!

Dynasty was triumphant . . . and shaken. It had never been accomplished so easily. Of course, this was only her third harvesting. Even so, it had seemed easy. Her gaze slanted toward Aaron outlined in the beam of the arc lamp that stayed lit all night. Some called the lamps, affixed high on the power pole, a farmer's night-light. There was a silvery cast to his features, as though they'd been sculpted by Mercury himself. That argent toughness had been visible all the while they picked, and with it was laughter between him and Dorothy or the workers. Somehow the amusement died when she and Aaron looked at each other.

No matter, she told herself. She had to admit Aaron had been the linchpin that had hooked the working machine consisting of him, Dorothy, four workers, and herself into organized, efficient speed.

Dorothy had been admiring. The workers had shown respect tinged with admiration. He'd worked right along with all of them, his body swinging from the waist in the seesaw motion that counterbalanced that gentle finger grabbing that marked a good picker. He joked, encouraged, sang off key, whistled, turning the job into rhythmic industry.

Dynasty didn't know how to thank him. Words couldn't do it. Her gratitude went too deep . . . and there was more. Aaron had gotten under her skin, causing inner tremors she'd never experienced. Sometimes he'd glance at her, and she'd discover she was holding her breath, as though anticipating . . . what? Whenever their eyes met, she felt like she'd been punched in the midsection. His emerald eyes would turn to green flame, touching her like fire. Even during her trial she hadn't felt as off balance as Aaron made her feel. It wasn't unpleasant. It was unsettling, unnerving. It had taken her so long to get control of her life, to begin charting her way. In a few days Aaron had managed to jog her loose of her sanity anchors. Sometimes she was sure she could spread her arms wide and fly.

Nonsense, she thought. She had to think rationally, about things like Honeysuckle Farm. It had been a fruitful harvest. If she got it to market virtually unscathed, she could continue to pay bills, some on time. She focused on the lake. The view was hidden in the darkness, but it didn't matter. She knew it by heart. It had been her salvation, her comfort, more than once. To the north crystal clean water, and beyond it, the hills, the distant, mystical drumlins. Even farther to the north, out of sight, the wondrous, breathtaking Adirondacks with their six million acres of park. Gazing at her vista was generally all it took to keep her level. Not now. She couldn't deny that Aaron had grown in her mind, filled the empty spaces, dried the agony stored there and turned it to dust. All her efforts to keep him out of her thoughts hadn't worked.

The picking and packing had been completed in five days, two days short of her goal. Each morning when she rose and fed the horses, Aaron would appear, with his crooked smile enveloping her like a tent. He was tough. Not just his strong muscled body, his quick mind, but more. Under that social patina was a man who knew who he was, who could be ruthless if the occasion arose. How she knew that, she couldn't guess. She was sure of it, though. How had he wormed his way into her brain and spirit? It was as though he'd always been at Honeysuckle Farm. At least he'd gotten the job done.

Dorothy had been elated. "He's a real country boy. Knows how to work. I like that."

Dynasty agreed. Not even to Dorothy had she been able to verbalize the other sensations he dredged out of her, the ones that'd made her palms sweat, her upper lip bead with moisture, her lower body throb with an alien beat. Awesome. She'd begun to like him as well. Not just his camaraderie with the workers and Dorothy, but his friendliness with her animals, the respect he showed them.

Now the work was done. It was time to go. Dorothy would stay behind this time and watch the animals, while Dynasty and Aaron drove to New York City. It made sense. Last harvest they hadn't had the mustangs. Dynasty told herself to think of it as just a business trip. Nothing more. Blasting herself with reason didn't prevent the watery, weak feeling behind her knees.

A reluctant smile lifted her lips as she watched Aaron check the load again, eye the sky, then approach her. "We should go," he said.

She glanced at the clouds that looked light blue against the navy background of night. The very bright summer moon shone on them like a beacon to light her way. The stars competed with the costliest diamonds and won hands down. In some subtle way she had the feeling that her life's way had arced in another direction, that the planets and firmament had shifted. Nothing drastic, but a subtle curve that shook her. "I'd like to be there at four-thirty," she said.

"Let's go." Aaron grinned at her in the beam from the overhead yard light. "You said it's a five- to six-hour drive into the heart of Manhattan?"

"Yes. To Green Market, as some call it. I've always called it the Union Square Market." She glanced at the truck, feeling steadier when she looked away from him. "It was good of Pepper to lend us his truck. Though it looks like an oversize wooden crate, and out of balance because of the high sides, our product will ride well.

"And that's damned important. Not a bruised one

in the bunch. The buyers will be pleased. Our gooseberries and blueberries are waited for, believe me. The two previous times we've taken them down, we've sold out. Last time we were bought out almost before we'd parked, let alone unloaded."

Aaron nodded. "Then let's roll. I'm more than willing to drive, but this is your baby, so you call it."

"You drive," Dorothy said, yawning.

Dynasty gazed at her.

"Don't look so annoyed, Dynasty. You can take your turn. As soon as you leave, I'm feeding those squalling cats and that wolf. Then I'm going back to bed. Harvesting is exhausting. It's eleven-thirty at night . . . two hours past my bedtime." She gave Dynasty a lopsided smile. "It's a damned good harvest. Even Pepper said so."

Dynasty hugged her. "Thanks."

"Thanks nothing. I'm getting my share." She kissed Dynasty's cheek. "Careful of the Kentuckian. He's no butter-'n-egg man, but he's got a look about him."

Dynasty blushed, glad the darkness covered it. Then she kissed her friend and climbed into the passenger seat of the outsize truck. "Thank Pepper for the truck. None of the berries will be damaged in this thing."

"If you don't turn over." Dorothy smothered another yawn and looked at the high, unwieldy wooden frame atop the back of Pepper's truck. "It looks mighty shaky."

"It'll do," Dynasty called out, waving.

"Hang on, Ms. Jones, we're on our way to market," Aaron told her. "So long, Dorothy."

Dorothy moved around to the driver's side, tapping Aaron's elbow where it rested on the door. "Be careful of her."

"I will."

"Good. She's gold."

"I agree." Aaron put it in gear, released the clutch, and they bounced down the driveway.

"What did Dorothy say to you?" Dynasty asked.

"She told me to take care of you. I said I would."

"Oh."

He smiled, checking the dimly lit dash. "I consider it a pleasure, ma'am."

"All that Southern charm." She tried to sound sarcastic. It came out breathy.

"I'm trying to impress you."

She ignored his throaty declaration and husky chuckle. "Thank you for helping us . . . and for driving too. I didn't expect—"

"I offered."

Dynasty took a deep breath as they turned onto the highway. It would be all right. She and Dorothy had driven it last time, changing drivers halfway. They'd been exhausted on the return trip, not figuring they had enough money to stay overnight in the Big Apple. This time she'd be even more tired from trying to figure out Aaron, and her responses to him. Ridiculous! She was an adult, who'd paid a big price to call her soul her own. No man could put her off balance.

He already has, a voice deep inside insisted.

She inhaled a shivery breath. The trip would be fine. She wouldn't be staying overnight in Manhattan with Aaron either. Even as she thought it, her mind conjured up just such a scenario. Her heart slammed against her breastbone. Don't think about that! "Tell me about Burcell Farms."

Aaron shot a look at her as he headed toward the interstate. They'd pick up the thruway at a place called Weedsport. "It's beautiful. Fenced pastureland for miles. Horses, young and old, large and small. I'd still like you to visit there with me."

She slanted a look at him. "I really don't know you that well, Aaron. You've mentioned this, but . . . I don't want to sound ungrateful—"

"You don't." He hit the wheel softly with his left hand. "How about a deal?"

"What kind of deal?"

He laughed. "Such a suspicious nature."

"I've learned . . . the hard way."

He sobered. "I'll bet." He shot her another glance. "I know you were innocent. I don't need any stats of yours to prove it. I've watched you with Dorothy and the people you hired to help you with the crop. They have faith in you. So do I."

"Thanks." Her smile slipped.

"Don't think about the past. You beat it. Remember?"

"I do." The straightforward way he reassured her brought a lump to her throat. "I—I still don't think I should go to Kentucky."

"About the deal . . ."

"All right. I'll listen."

"If all goes well here, if you sell your harvest as you hope to, fast and complete, let me buy you breakfast, and we can talk about a trip to Kentucky. On the way to the city, I'll tell you about my parents and their home, where you'd be staying, and about my siblings. There's plenty of them too."

Dynasty caught the assurance, the veiled promise that he wasn't about to lure her into anything. She took a deep breath. "We can have something to eat . . . if the deal goes well. I'll buy since you've worked so hard for Honeysuckle Farm."

"I didn't do it for the farm, Dynasty. I did it for you. No sense pretending."

Warmth curled through her. "You move fast." She was having a hard time breathing. That hadn't happened to her once when she was on trial. Aaron Burcell made her dizzy.

"It looks that way . . . maybe." He glanced her way. "Don't shut the door, yet, let me make a case."

"Now, you're a lawyer."

He laughed. "No. I'm a businessman."

"In horses."

"Yes."

"And the grass doesn't grow under your feet. No maybe about it."

"I'm interested in you. I won't deny it."

She smiled into the night lighted by the headlights that gave a tunnel effect to their journey. She was interested too. Did they give the same meaning to the words? She couldn't afford to be wrong about him. A sixth sense told her she could be pulverized by Aaron.

They turned onto the interstate that would take them into Auburn, then from there to Weedsport. He was making good time. "I have the horse you want," she said.

"There's that, plus the need to prove that I treat animals fairly and humanely."

"I don't need a trip to Kentucky for that. I've watched you with Lupe while we picked, and during your lunch breaks, I saw how you were with the mustangs, and Stormy, and the kittens."

He chuckled. "It isn't hard to be kind to animals, Dynasty. I've never known a period in my life when they weren't part of it. We have woods on the farms with every sort of bird including raptors."

"We have hawks and eagles." She caught his surprise. "They nest in the Montezumas, a huge swamp and wildlife preserve about twenty miles north of the farm."

"I've heard of the preserve. Never been there. Have you?"

Dynasty nodded, feeling more lighthearted than she had in a long time. "Dorothy and I canoed through a portion of it last summer, after the black fly season. It's wonderful."

"Show it to me sometime."

A fluttery sensation shivered over her. Had he just suggested he'd be back to the area? "There're game preserve people who—"

"I'd rather you showed me."

Silence stretched between them. Companionable. Dynasty couldn't figure why all the inferences he made didn't bother her, or make her want to stay out of his way. She was cautious, but not one bit repelled. That had been her usual response to anything that smacked of a come-on in the last few years. Aaron Burcell elicited far different reactions from her.

"I've told my family about you," he said.

"You have?" Dynasty was flummoxed.

"How smart you are, how resourceful and quick-minded. As an afterthought I told them you were beautiful."

Dynasty swallowed, feeling as though the cab of the truck had shrunk to half its size. Her heart labored in her chest. She looked out the side window at the fading starlight, wishing on one. She needed endurance and problem solving, O Daystar. The summer moon paled as they turned left down the country road leading to the thruway. At the tollgate they took their ticket, exchanged quick pleasantries with the attendant, and were on their way.

Aaron felt her slide in her seat belt and knew without looking that Dynasty was asleep. He glanced at her, smiling, then looked at the sky. Soon the grayness of predawn would come, then the dawn. They had to be in Manhattan before then. He increased his speed, not tired, liking the feel of the heavy truck, determined to go the distance rather than wake her.

He opened his side vent on the vintage truck, just enough to give him a breeze, not enough to disturb Dynasty. Even though it was still night, his instincts told him it was going to be a blinding, burning day. The muted roar of the engine, the swish of the few passing cars had a salubrious effect. He glanced at Dynasty again. It was just as well she was asleep. He had a great deal to ponder.

When he'd taken on the job of rooting out the rumors of Moonstruck being enclosed in a mustang herd, he'd never considered he would run smack-dab into his future. His anger had brought him to New York. The death of Casey, his mentor since childhood, father of his friend Rory, the disappearance of a prime horse, had catapulted him to Yokapa County.

Violet eyes and red hair had kept him there. He glanced at Dynasty, then back at the road. She was a prickly lady who was more beautiful than anything he'd seen in his life. There'd been lovely women before, in Kentucky . . . New York City . . . Dublin . . . Los Angeles. Some had captured his interest. None had crawled through his blood into his nervous system like Dynasty Jones. At first sight, with her face flushed, her hair riddled with straw, dressed in old denim, she'd laid him low, excited him. She continued to do so. Was it her features? A straight nose, slightly retrousse. Not uncommon. Skin like fresh cream with a hint of coral. Damn! A horseman turning poetic? It wasn't hard when talking about Dynasty.

He sensed her wariness and understood it. As

much as he would like to leap over every barrier around her and knock down the rest, he couldn't. She needed to be wooed . . . with truth. His desire told him to rush his fences, clutch her to him and never let go. The man who loved her urged caution.

Love? How was that possible? He'd figured it took years, even though his father had told him innumerable times he had known he loved his Mel on first sight.

Aaron chuckled, then muffled it when Dynasty stirred. What would she say if he woke her and proposed? Probably push him out of the truck and continue on to Manhattan by herself. He wasn't so stupid that he didn't know the attraction between them was strong, that Dynasty felt it too. She just hadn't burst into flames yet as he had.

There was the rub. How to convince her, and not act like a panting stallion in heat. He winced at the comparison. He could picture the horror in her eyes, the rejection. She'd been hurt by a host of coworkers, women and men she'd believed she could trust. Her trust had been smashed, disintegrated and washed away like a sand castle. Could he rebuild it? Maybe. But not fast. No crashing at the gates for Dynasty. First he'd prove his friendship, then his ardor would follow.

He gritted his teeth. Could he hold out?

He glanced at the sleeping Dynasty, a smile curving his mouth. His life had changed in a matter of days. Now he had his work cut out for him. Convincing her that they would be good together was going to take time and effort. More than worth it. His smile widened. He wasn't about to let her get away.

Dynasty had the sensation of sailing. She'd never known it could be so pleasant. Something wasn't right, though. She should've been doing something else. She opened her eyes, frowning, letting the world settle around her. She wasn't on the water. She was in Pepper's big truck . . . next to Aaron Burcell.

She watched his hands on the wheel. He drove well. Where were they? She scoured the area with her eyes. Lord! It was still dark, but she knew hours had elapsed. He'd driven more than halfway. She eyed him again, thankful for the silver beams of passing autos. Silver warrior. Strange word for a modern businessman. Yet it fit. He was like a champion of old who'd come to her assistance. The boon he asked was a trip to Kentucky. Her mouth went dry when she thought of it.

She'd changed in the short time they'd known each other. Somehow her past had shrunk. Though it could never be insignificant, it had certainly dropped from huge importance. He'd given her relief from the pain. The keystone of her humiliation had disintegrated, turned to dust. She could view it as a sad learning experience. Three months ago, she couldn't have. Not even four weeks ago.

She took a deep breath. "I'll drive now, Aaron."

His head slewed her way, and he grinned, his

teeth flashing in the dimness. "It's fine. I enjoy driving."

"So do I," she said, not giving way. "It's my job. I want to do my part."

"The next rest area's coming up. I'll get gas, then you can drive. I'd like to check the tires anyway."

Dynasty stiffened. "Do you think the tires are bad?"

"Nope. I just want to keep a constant pressure with this load. Better safe than sorry."

She exhaled. "Yes. Right. We could get some coffee too."

"Good idea." He smiled at her.

Two and a half hours later, Aaron at the wheel again, they made their way into the stop-and-go traffic of Manhattan. The sky had turned pewter, with a pale coral glow seaming the bottom.

"It's a little after four-thirty, but not much," he said.

"We made it," Dynasty said. They were almost there! On time! She eyed the man next to her. Though he made it look effortless, his concentration was on driving. It gave her ample opportunity to study him. He was a tall, beautiful man. Caring. Very sexy. Strange, she mused. She hadn't wanted to think about a man that way in some time. She hadn't missed that aspect of living, nor had she sought it. Now it was on her mind a good share of the time. Let's face it. Since the advent of Aaron Burcell, she'd thought of little else. Maybe it was nutty, but that was the way it was. She smiled. Wellness had come with

Burcell? Maybe it wasn't that black-and-white, but he'd sure made a difference.

"So what have you decided, Dynasty?"

She jerked her head around to look forward, then at him again. "That for a Kentuckian, you're not half bad."

He laughed, steering around a cab, ignoring the blowing horns. "I'll take it." He pointed. "Is that the market? Where the trucks are turning?"

"Yes." She leaned forward, excitement filling her. *Manhattan, I'm back again.* She exhaled, smiling. *My head's up, and I'm not afraid.*

Getting to the parking place she directed Aaron to, took time. Dynasty was pleased when more than one buyer waved to her and followed the truck to the spot. "Hello, Mr. Hirschmeyer. How's business?"

"It could be better . . . maybe not too much." He grinned, his gold tooth showing, and Dynasty laughed.

The next three hours were hectic. Aaron dived into the shouting bidding that was friendly, good-natured, and serious, as though he was a born auctioneer. At the end of the selling, Dynasty took her money to the nearest branch of her bank, deposited it, then walked over to Aaron, smiling.

He straightened, his smile answering hers. When she waved her deposit slip, he chuckled. "You did well, Dynasty Jones."

"We did," she corrected him. She bit her lip. "I want to pay you—"

He put one finger on her lips, shaking his head.

"I'm proving myself, Dynasty. Let's have that breakfast. I'm starved."

"So am I." And she was. She hadn't been this hungry in a long time.

Over hotcakes for her, eggs over medium with hash browns, crisp bacon, and homemade rye bread toast for him, they talked little, smiled a great deal.

At last Aaron sat back, sipping his coffee. "That was good."

"Mine too."

"What did Dorothy say when you called?"

"She whooped when I told her that I got twenty cents a pint more than last year."

"You're pleased."

She nodded. "I can pay off a few debts, buy some things I need, and still have a bank account. Not bad."

He put down his cup, rested his elbows on the table, and leaned toward her. "Sounds good. So come with me to Kentucky, lady. I can show you more about me than just my berry-picking skills. I want you to see it all. What do you say?"

A protest trembled on her lips. Forget it, Aaron. Go on your way. That was prudent. The words rose up and stuck in her throat. Not seeing him again would hurt . . . a lot.

"Don't say no."

His warm eyes showed concern, anxiousness. She wanted to reach out to him, hold his hand. Instead she took a deep breath and spoke. "All right. I won't."

SIX

Horses! Miles of them. More white fences than she'd thought there were on earth. It almost distracted her enough to blot out the worry and concern about being in Kentucky with Aaron. How had she let herself be talked into it? He'd made it sound so plausible. Dorothy had been so encouraging. Kentucky! Good Lord. She had a farm to run . . . even if the summer harvest was in.

"What do you think?" Aaron asked. They'd gotten out of his car and were looking over the pastures that seemed to stretch for miles, squared off by leagues of white fencing.

"It's wonderful. I've never seen anything like it, or so many beautiful animals all together." It was an extravaganza of horses of all sizes. They raced, they ran, they gamboled, they cozied up to one another, neighed, whinnied, almost laughed out loud.

He laughed. "I knew you'd like it. That pleases

me." His eyes slitted in concentration as he studied the panoply of horses. "I love it."

Dynasty's stomach jumped into her throat. She forced it down and turned to him, a smile in place. "You're like this place, Aaron Burcell. Smooth as fresh butter, as my Amish friend Jacob Meistersaenger would say."

He touched her cheek with one finger, letting it trace down from forehead to chin.

"What?" Her voice was breathy, sketchy.

"You've become a habit, Dynasty. I've got to be with you. Go figure, as they say in New York. Think you'll ever use my first name . . . all by itself?"

"Sure I will, and have . . . Aaron Burcell."

He laughed and slipped an arm around her waist. "Forget it, lady. You couldn't get me mad today if you backed the car over me."

"Care to test that theory?"

He grinned and leaned down, his face close to hers. "Bloodthirsty, aren't you?"

"Why aren't you running, instead of standing here, grinning?"

"I've attained a great objective, Dynasty."

"What's that?" She couldn't get the squeak out of her voice.

"You're here. I wanted you to see it, to believe in me."

The simple declaration rocked her. She could tell it surprised him that he'd said it. His deprecatory shrug didn't water down the words. If anything it magnified them. Dynasty had to swallow twice before she answered. "Just because of Stormy. The deal is—"

"If you see that the horses are well cared for, not abused or misused in any way, I can borrow Moonstruck . . . Stormy for races and, in a few years, for stud purposes."

Dynasty nodded. "Agreed. Oh. Look at the baby—"

"Foal. That's one of Kiltie Dea's through Aaron's Delight."

Dynasty slanted him a glance. "Named after you, Daddy?"

"Sorry. This one isn't after me. I know how anxious you are to prove a relationship between myself and the horses, especially their backsides."

Dynasty laughed. "You're right about that."

"Not this time. My grandfather is Aaron too. The best horseman in this country, according to a great many people besides myself."

"Aaron one and two?"

Aaron shook his head, moving closer to her. "He's called Buzz. He wouldn't allow any shortened names on his horses, but he's called by one. Buzz O'Farrell from Ireland. He brought two steeplechasers from there, thinking to start the sport here. Instead he married a horse farmer's daughter. Their daughter, my mother, married my father, J. Douglas Burcell, who's now owner of Burcell Farms, and who's called Doogie." Aaron grinned when she looked questioning. "The Burcells are Scottish and

Irish. They shorten names. At least they do in our family."

"But not your name."

He shook his head. "My mother wouldn't allow it." He looked at the farm. "My dad bought this place from my grandfather, then enlarged it as each Burcell arrived." He lifted some soil from the ground, crumpling it in his hands. "When my father married my mother, he was still at Cornell studying animal husbandry. That was my field at the university. After one year, I changed to business. As much as I like horses and want to continue to raise them, I find the business end just as interesting—"

"Is the house very old?"

He nodded. "Once it was just a cabin." He waved his arm. "And this was all going to be a vegetable farm. My great-great-grandfather bought it, built stables, bought horses. After that he began taking care of the house." He smiled at her. "It's plain, but I think it's pretty special."

"How many horses do you have?"

"About fifty, sometimes less or more. We trade, sell, and buy, building the stock, strengthening it."

"Have they raced at Churchill Downs?"

He smiled, nodding. "So you know about the Kentucky Derby?"

"What American doesn't? It's a spring classic."

"It is. And yes, we've had some runners in it, and the Preakness and Belmont Stakes as well. Our big winner was Saltee Sam—"

"I've heard of that horse!"

"A Triple Crown winner. Our only one so far. But we've won some great races with other horses."

"Is Stormy one?"

"He hasn't done any big racing, but, yes, he has great potential. Very strong, and never seems to tire."

Dynasty laughed. "Yes. He's like that."

Aaron turned to look at her, his one finger stroking her cheek. "And you rode him."

She nodded.

"You're some lady, Dynasty Jones." He took her arm, leading her back to the car. "My family is going to love you . . . too."

Her heart flipped in her chest. What was he saying? "I don't think so."

He tucked her into the car and closed the door. "Sure they will." He went around the hood of the car.

Dynasty took deep breaths. This wasn't a good idea. She shouldn't have come to Kentucky. *Keep your head. Stand your ground.* Those maxims rolled through her mind, much as they had when she'd been on trial. She'd never be put on the spot again. She turned to him when he entered the car. "Aaron, I—"

"Let's not argue. We've come here to look at the horses. Right?"

"Yes, but—"

"Then, let's do that. We can put everything else on hold until we're back in Yokapa County. Right?"

"I suppose." Had he said when "we're" back?

Instead of starting the car, he laid his arm along

the back of the seat. "Do you take Lupe riding in the car with you?"

"What? Lupe? Ah . . . yes. Most of the time she stays home. She's good that way. If she's not taken, she resigns herself to remaining on the farm. She rarely wanders. On short trips I always take her. She seems to love riding." She was babbling! He made her crazy.

"I'll bet you don't lock your door when you leave her in the car."

"No. People are honest in Yokapa County."

"Damned afraid of a wolf, too, if they're smart." Annoyed, Dynasty looked out her window.

"For a woman who dislikes animals—"

"Unacquainted with them is a better description. We moved too much when I was growing up. There wasn't an opportunity to get a pet. To be truthful, I don't recall missing it."

His glance caught the arrested expression on her face. "You just remembered something. A puppy?"

"No. Once I had a pigeon. I found him hurt. I was able to keep him until he could fly again. Then we were posted to Georgia." She hadn't thought of that in ages.

"Your voice had a hollow sound, as though it surprised you to recall that."

She licked her lips, feeling defensive. "You're probing, Burcell."

"We're back to last names. Annoyed?"

"No, *Aaron*, I'm not."

"Good." He turned the key, then put the car in

gear, keeping to the ten mile an hour speed limit prescribed for the miles of lanes on Burcell property. "I admit I'd like to know more about Dynasty Jones."

"Find a newspaper morgue. Go back a few years. There's plenty on me." She hadn't made remarks like that to many people. Such sarcasm had been tested on Dorothy, and only her, until Aaron had showed up. He was irksome . . . but he was stalwart. The trip to New York proved that. They'd crossed a bridge then. Strange! It must've been his offhandedness that disarmed her. It seemed natural to mention that dark time of her life to Aaron.

Aaron swerved and braked to avoid a duck crossing the road with some of her ducklings. He leaned on the wheel, grinning, allowing the slow entourage time to get to the other side. "Sorry, Emmaline," he called out the window.

"A tenant?" Dynasty laughed when the mother duck turned and quacked loudly at them. "I think you made an enemy."

"I'd make thousands of them to hear that."

The hushed words shivered over her. Confused, she turned toward him. "Hear what?"

"Your laugh. You have a dimple right here." One hand touched the corner of her mouth.

Heart racing, Dynasty looked away, scrambling for something to say that wouldn't sound as though she were falling apart. She was.

"I'd like you to tell me about yourself, Dynasty . . . and not about the fiasco on Wall Street. You and I both know you were innocent."

If it hadn't been for the car door, she would've fallen out on the gravel drive. Not one person but Dorothy had ever manifested so much faith in her about the past. Not even Dynasty herself. She swallowed twice. "Maybe . . . in time I'll tell you."

"Fair enough."

When he started the car with a slight jerk, she braced one hand against the dashboard.

"Sorry," he said. "I guess I'm excited about bringing you home."

She swallowed. "I like your car. It's like the rental you drove to the farm."

His grin widened. "Change the subject? Okay. I can do that." He slapped the wheel of his classic Porsche. "This baby needs a tuning, wheel balancing, oil change, and general cosmetic surgery. But I like it. It's not new, but it has class."

"Ah, not just horses, but cars are your specialty as well." She'd begun to breathe normally again, but what he'd said to her wouldn't be forgotten. There was a special file in her mind for Aaron.

His smile twisted. "I'm not bragging, Dynasty. My parents believed in *tuning up* their children. Before we could drive, we had to be able to dismantle a car and put it back together . . . correctly."

"How many are in your family?"

"Six. Two brothers. Three sisters. All married and living in Kentucky."

"How homey." She bit her lip. "I didn't mean that the way it sounded."

"You sounded . . . wishful." He put out his

hand when she stiffened. "Don't do that. I can feel you tensing again. Maybe I'm clumsy with you, because I see a different Dynasty Jones than you do."

"You don't know me."

"I want to."

"So do I," she muttered, barely noticing his surprised glance. At first she'd been so intent on clearing her name, she'd let no other thoughts in her mind. When it was over, she'd been too drained to talk to anyone except her lawyer, Dee Brown. They'd become friends because of common goals and beliefs. The business end of being a lawyer, and being the accused, had segued into a strong friendship. Dee had given up private practice not long after the trial to join a law firm in Washington, D.C. There were only long distance calls between them now. Both tried to keep them upbeat.

So, in essence, until she'd gone to Yokapa County and Dorothy, she'd had few shoulders to cry on, no stalwart defender. Rather than wallow in what she didn't have, Dynasty had thrown herself into leaving Manhattan. She could still recall that deep sense of loss, the need to talk. Thank heavens she'd found Dorothy and Honeysuckle Farm. She owed Dee a call. Her lawyer friend had promised to visit Yokapa County one day.

"Ruminating?" Aaron asked.

"Pardon?"

"You were in a blue funk, Dynasty. Bad thoughts?"

"Not really. I was thinking of my lawyer."

"You had a good one?"

"The best."

He leaned over and caught her hand, squeezing it. "Good. You deserve the best." He stopped the car again. "Look."

"Oh. It's beautiful."

"That's the main house."

Dynasty had expected grandeur. Instead she saw a big homey, structure that resembled a giant comfortable pile. It glistened, welcoming, in the sun. Stone, cream and brown with clapboard, dark green shutters, wide, deep, high windows. Natural cedar double doors at the front. Brass fittings winked from every corner. Instead of the usual white fence, the one around the house was cream to match the stone and clapboard. "It's a postcard. Beautiful."

"I like it. Plenty of room."

"It's big . . . but friendly."

"Like me," Aaron whispered.

She turned her head, and their faces almost met. "Trust me, Dynasty," he murmured.

Dynasty didn't have time to ponder Aaron's words, to wonder if she could ever trust again. As soon as Aaron had parked his car, people seemed to come out of the woodwork. She met the trainers, the groundskeepers, swampers, the farm jockeys, house staff . . . and the family. She'd never met such an outspoken group.

"You have Moonstruck." A sleekly garbed woman

in chestnut half boots and umber stretch pants, threw the words at her in breathy accusation.

"I own a horse named Stormy . . . who resembles one called Moonstruck."

The woman inclined her head. "I'm Terry, Aar's older sister." She gestured to a cluster of men. "That's my husband, Tony Balland. Next to him is Noah, our brother. He's younger than Aar. Aaron and I are the oldest. After Noah comes Clare, then Rita and Jody. Jody's a boy. Clear?"

"As mud," Dynasty rejoined.

A small smile lighted Terry's austere features. "You might do."

"You might not." Lifting her chin Dynasty moved around the older sister, looking for Aaron. Her stomach felt like jelly. So did her knees. Stand your ground, she told herself, chin up, shoulders back. Hadn't Gramma Peabody always said that? No one was walking on her again!

Aaron touched her arm, his face creased in concern. "All right?"

"Yes."

The man Terry had pointed out as her husband moved up next to them, one arm around Terry. "Wow! Aar, you brought home a toughie. My wife's mouth is hanging open." Tony Balland grinned at his scowling spouse. "Been bested, love?"

"Yes." She punched him in the arm, but allowed him to kiss her.

Aaron turned around, smiling. "I should've warned you, Ter. Don't mess with the New Yorker.

She'll take you down." His grin widened when he turned back to a red-faced Dynasty. "What did you say to my quick-tongued older sibling?" He caught her hand, closing his fingers around hers when she would've wrenched free.

"Nothing."

"She told me she didn't think I would do when I said she might," Terry sang out.

When the family and others laughed, Dynasty took a deep breath. It surprised her to see the wealth of goodwill on everyone's faces. An older man, straight-backed, skin weathered with humor and the elements, approached.

"My children getting to you?" he asked. He put out his hand. "I'm Doogie Burcell, father rooster to this brood of chicks. Pay them no mind. They've been out of control since birth. I've taken bullwhips to them, dropped them off cliffs. Nothing works. Someone once suggested backing a truck over them, but I didn't want to ruin the undercarriage."

"Good plan." Dynasty forgot her wariness when he laughed. It boomed out of him.

A diminutive woman in jodhpurs and boots came up next to him. "Pay my husband no mind, Dynasty. Welcome to Burcell Farms. We want you to be happy here. I'm Amelia O'Farrell Burcell, mother to this gaggle of giants. Delighted you're with us."

When she leaned up and kissed her cheek, Dynasty's knees buckled. "How do you do, Mrs. Burcell?"

"Call me Mel, dear. Everyone does, don't they, Doogie?"

"They do, m'love. Tell her the truth. You run the farm and everybody on it, including me."

"Especially you."

Dynasty felt like she was in a fast-forward video. Everyone talked and laughed at once, commented, chuckled, riposted . . . all without seeming to take a breath. The Burcells were formidable. If this was the all-American family, then the world should duck.

"I'm sorry you're going to be here such a short time," Mel said, "but we'll do our best to make it a happy one. We're having a little cookout in three days, Dynasty, to welcome you to the family."

"I beg your pardon?" At Mel's widening smile, Dynasty almost choked. "Now, look. I . . . I think you should know—"

"She's delighted at your warm welcome, Mother."

Dynasty spun toward Aaron. "Wait a minute—"

"Isn't that sweet? She stands right up to Aar." Mel patted her hand. "It's by far the best way to handle them. Oh, this is one of our other daughters."

"Hi. I'm Clare Burcell Dunphy, a younger sister to Aar. My husband's Sean. He's from Ireland."

Tall, stunning, and sharp was Dynasty's first impression of Aaron's dark-haired, dark-eyed sibling. "Hi."

Another woman reached around Clare, putting out her hand. "I agree with Mama. Put 'em in their place. Hi, I'm Marguerite Burcell Lyman." She pointed. "That's my husband, Max. We do most of the training on the farm." She grinned. "Everyone calls me Rita."

"How . . . are . . . you . . . ?" Dynasty backed a step.

"Aaron told us you called him Aaron Burcell for the longest time. Cute. Why'd you do it?"

"Ah . . . I don't know."

"Aar, have you intimidated this woman?" Rita looked up at her brother.

"Certainly not," Dynasty said, then reddened when they laughed. She swallowed, her confused gaze swinging to Aaron.

He grinned and put an arm around her waist. "Dynasty sets her own rules for things . . . even names."

"She's nailed him," Clare said with clear enjoyment.

"So she has," Terry drawled, moving to her sister's side.

"I love it," Rita breathed.

"Ladies, back off. Hi, Dynasty Jones. I'm Noah. This is Jody. Welcome to our family."

Dynasty stared at one after another of the grinning faces, before she looked up at Aaron.

He kissed her nose. "They're just welcoming you."

"I see." But she didn't. They were too fast, too close . . . like Aaron, who'd become an intimate in just days. What would this cost her? Had she let him get under her guard? For a moment she panicked as though the world was sliding out from under her. She took deep breaths, promising herself that no one could control her life but her.

SEVEN

Aaron stared in the mirror of the guest bedroom he always used when he stayed at the main house. Damn! he thought. Dynasty was more beautiful here than she'd been on her own farm. Her chin was always up, her gaze challenging. Behind it he could see the defensiveness, the bandaged hurt, the still oozing wound of being thought without honor when honor had driven her every venture. In his time he'd come across varying types of people, differing levels of integrity. He'd been fooled, but not by the same type twice. He'd become a fairly accurate judge of character. With Dynasty Jones, he'd felt no need to reflect, to judge, to weigh any conceptions or preconceptions. He knew, and he'd known at once. She was a pillar of goodness. Every instinct told him to trust her.

With all that virtue that coated her like second skin, she was the sexiest, the hottest, the most desirable female who'd ever passed his way. Accepting that had been easier than he'd figured. His life had made a one eighty, and he'd adjusted in one smooth moment of meeting. He was hers. Wondering when he'd tell her didn't take great conjecture. Knowing that he'd feel the right time, that he'd know the moment, was a surety. How would she take it? He laughed.

"What's funny?"

Aaron didn't even start. "That was always the danger."

"Meaning?"

"As a father, you were always too quick, quiet, and fast."

"Had to be. That's how I got your mother."

Aaron's gaze moved from his father's mirrored image to his own. Maybe that was the ticket with Dynasty. Her barriers were so high and deep, it was hard to get around, under, or over them. Didn't matter. He wouldn't give up. She was everything he'd ever hoped to meet or see.

"You didn't even hear me come in, son, because you had something on your mind. Or is it someone? Guess you were thinking about the pretty Northerner. She make you laugh?"

Aaron's eyes flashed at his father's reflection. "Doogie, you were always too nosy."

His father shrugged, grinning. "Can't help it. My job. What were you thinking about?"

"About her calling me a horse's ass first time she met me."

Doogie put back his head, his laughter booming

around the room. "She's a corker." He inclined his head. "Think she'll fit in with the horse crowd?"

"I don't give a damn. She's head and shoulders over the lot of them," Aaron said, his curt tone slicing at argument.

Doogie's grin widened. "Finally. Never thought it'd happen to you. Daisy Crumbaugh is going to be upset. Your mother tells me your old flame Arledge is back too. Took back the Gaines name, as well. Daisy marked you for her own. Arledge might too. This could be a real chuckle." He laughed. "I recognize that look on your face. Mine was like that when Mel's papa challenged my intentions. 'Course they were strictly dishonorable. He'd read me right."

Aaron turned around. "Grandpa O'Farrell liked you," he said, glad to change the subject.

"'Cause I married her. And I was glad he insisted on it. He was worried about the hot stuff between us. I was more concerned about losing her. Wasn't about to let anybody else have her." He leaned against the dresser. "Dynasty Jones. She's quality. Any fool could see it. I know all about her. I saw her on television. Some people we know won't think she's quality. I do."

"I don't give a damn what anyone thinks," Aaron said through his teeth. His smile was stony. "Even you, Doogie. Though I'm glad you can see how classy she is. Anybody, including family members, says a word against her, they go up against me."

Doogie grinned. "That's good enough for me, boy. She's more'n welcome to this family."

Aaron's smile twisted. "Don't count on that. She has a mind of her own . . . and it's not leaning in my favor at the moment."

"You got her here. Change her mind."

"I intend to try." He frowned. "She's been punched and kicked, Doogie. I don't like it."

"It's up to you to battle alongside her, then." He nodded, once. "I'll back the two of you."

Aaron laughed. "I'm halfway home." He frowned again.

"What now?"

"I can't get over the feeling she isn't out of the woods."

Doogie straightened. "I hope you're not saying she's at risk on Burcell Farms."

Aaron shook his head. "I don't know. Just a feeling I have . . ."

"You get that from your mother's side. Scottish and Lakota Sioux in her blood. Strange combination. Both sides of the O'Farrell family always had precognition."

Aaron eyed his parent. "I didn't know you believed in that."

"Don't tell your mother. I like to tease her about it." He slapped his son on the back. "Make your move, any way you want. I'll be there."

Aaron shook his father's hand. "I guess I always knew that."

❖———————❖

"Dorothy? Hi. How are things—?"

"This is a collect call, Dynasty. Talk fast. You haven't the loose change for this sort of thing."

"I'll get an eight hundred number." She paused. "You sound out of sorts. Is everything all right?"

"Yes. Strange thing, though. Yesterday, you had a call. Since I'm staying here instead of my place, I picked it up on the first ring. Somebody asked for you. I said you weren't here. They asked if you were at Burcell Farms. I said, who wants to know? They hung up."

Dynasty conquered the shivery feeling, calling on her mantra. Courage. It allowed her to empty herself of fear, let her mind focus on Dorothy and not the choking past. "No name?"

"Nothing else. I didn't recognize the voice. Don't be worried. I'm not. We can handle anything."

"I'm not there. You're alone. Keep Lupe in the house with you, anyway." She swallowed. "Dorothy, I want you to promise you'll call Jacob Meistersaenger and Pepper Lally. Tell them about the call. Jacob's sons and Pepper's strong arms would be a big help if a problem occurs."

"I'm all right—"

"Promise."

"Fine. I think you're making something big out of nothing. Come to think of it, I could bring in Stormy. He'd scare the pants off any intruder."

"Cleaning up after him could be a chore."

"Naw. Road apples never bothered me."

"It could create quite an aura in the house." Dynasty knew that Dorothy was trying to divert her. Going along with it didn't negate her concern. "You could be in danger."

"Tell me about it. Stormy could kick the house down."

"You know what I mean."

Dorothy sighed. "I'll talk to Jacob and Pepper."

"I'm coming back as soon as possible."

"Don't rush. I've paid the bills, yours and mine. I'm making jam with the damaged berries, plus some vinegars for the winter. The tomatoes are coming in by the thousands. I've taken some to the Meistersaengers' stand. I'm freezing the rest."

"I'll still worry."

Dynasty held the phone in her hand, even after she'd broken the connection. Who would be calling her and asking if she was at Burcell Farms? Who in Yokapa County would know or care where she was besides Dorothy? Telling herself it was nothing, that her troubles were behind her, didn't wash away the cold dampness on her skin. Nothing or no one could rain on her parade again. She'd paid her dues, proved to the world she wasn't a lawbreaker. Fear was a reflexive thing. It came on like a dark cloak when any negative button was pressed. It was nothing more. Forget it.

The knock on her door shook her free of her introspection. "Yes?"

"Aren't you ready, yet?"

She recognized Aaron's voice. "Go away. Dinner isn't for another hour."

"Open the door and talk to me. I'm bored."

She chuckled. He sounded like his face was pressed to the door. "I won't, little boy. On your way."

"You're mean, Dynasty Jones. I'd let you into my room."

"I'll bet you would." She was laughing.

"Yes, yes. Open the door. I'll take you there."

"No. I just got off the phone with Dorothy—"

"How is she? I hope you didn't call collect. Open the door and tell me what she said."

"Uh-uh. Sorry."

"Let's see. What's my next argument? Would you like to hear the story of my life? Open the door and I'll tell you."

"Your mother already did."

"She doesn't know the juicy stuff."

"I'll pass."

A big sigh coming through the door made her smile.

"I'll see you downstairs in half an hour," he said. "We'll have a drink and talk."

"Bye."

EIGHT

Dynasty expected jeans and boots. It was a family dinner, not a dress affair. Aaron had told her anything she wore would be suitable. She'd asked his sister Clare what was acceptable. She'd said dressy slacks, a skirt, anything comfortable. The family did look at ease in their garb. There were boots, shiny, ebony, chestnut, hand sewn. The jeans were hand-crafted as well and made of suede, leather, and silk that imitated the look of denim. Ties were eclectic—tied bows, string, Jerry Garcia originals on males and females. Aaron's mother wore silk culottes. Clare wore airy suede and smooth satin. Aaron, his brothers, and father had donned cotton shirts loomed as fine as a silkworm could do, in every hue of the spectrum. Dynasty had been too long in Manhattan not to recognize Madison Avenue casual, Milan leisure wear, Parisian cut. It was as though the Burcells had bent over backward to be plain and succeeded in looking sassily sophisticated.

Terry wore half boots with bejeweled heels. The women's understated jewelry looked like costume stuff. Dynasty was sure it wasn't. It didn't take a lapidary to recognize diamonds in shapes of spurs, whips, boots, horses. Dynasty smiled at the tailored posh effect.

"Something amuses you."

She knew it was Aaron without turning. "Yes. I don't think the average family dresses like this for dinner."

He looked around with an exaggerated expression of disbelief. "Really?"

She laughed, and he moved closer to her, his upper arm grazing her shoulder. "You're beautiful, Dynasty Jones. A vision in cream suede-cotton. I particularly like the fringe on your split skirt." He leaned down and whispered, "Very sexy."

She took a step back, trying not to blush.

"You know a great deal about fashion and fabric?"

"Sisters."

"Oh." She was sure it was more than that. She almost said it, until she saw his glance skate the room. "What's wrong? Why the scowl?"

"A horse is missing."

She stiffened.

He looked down at her. "Relax. It happens from time to time."

"You're worried."

He pressed his lips together. "I guess I am."

"Could the horse just be in another place on the farm? You said it's a large holding."

"It is, and it could be that. We'll know in a few hours. People are scouring the place now."

"Maybe we could help."

He stared down at her. "Thanks. I appreciate that."

"I . . . I don't want the horse to be missing." She shook her head. "You know what I mean."

"I do."

He was putting her into a tizzy—a pleasurable one. It was those damned eyes of his. When he leaned down and kissed her cheek, she saw stars and couldn't get enough air. "Your family," she murmured. "Don't want to draw attention."

"Too late. Every head turned when you walked down those stairs."

Disbelieving, she stared up at him.

"Honest, Dynasty. I thought I'd have to pop my brother Jody."

"Ridiculous."

"That's what I thought . . . and I told them that."

Mouth agape, she couldn't tear her gaze from him. "Horse," she managed in a wheeze.

He looked puzzled. "You want to go riding?"

"No." She cleared her throat. "We should look."

His arm tightened on her waist. "We'll wait." He leaned down and kissed her again. "You're compassionate. I like that."

"Tha-thank you."

"Polite too."

"Tell me about the horse."

"I'd rather talk about us."

"There isn't an 'us.' "

"Sure there is. You're just slower to catch on to it than I am."

"Thank you for that."

"You're welcome."

"You're polite, too . . . when you want to be."

"Yep. Actually I'd like to be alone with you." He grinned at her. "Let's crash out of here and—"

"No. We can't do that."

"All right. Let's go steady."

"Have you been drinking?"

"A little beer."

"People don't go steady anymore."

"Well, if you want to, we can be married right away. But, I'm sure my family would prefer—"

"You know I didn't mean that!"

Heads turned, curiosity on more than one face.

"You know I didn't mean that," Dynasty repeated, lowering her voice.

"Is this our first fight?" he asked.

"You should've been a lawyer," she said through her teeth. "You have an unerring eye for the jugular."

He shook his head. "I'm just pushing your buttons, because I can keep your attention on me that way." He grinned. "But I would marry you in a minute if you said yes."

Flummoxed, she took deep breaths. "I don't think your family would approve of—"

"I think it's time you got over what happened to you. Not forget it, but stop putting yourself on the stand every day. You might be the only person who thinks you weren't found innocent."

"I assure you there're a number of those." His words penetrated. "I did . . . do think I'm innocent."

"Good. Show 'em what you're made of." He ran his finger down her cheek. "And that time there was no bitterness in your voice."

Dynasty opened her mouth, then closed it. She cleared her throat. "There's one person who would've wanted me hanged."

His mouth lifted in a grim smile. "That's obvious. The person who set you up. Any idea who that was?"

She shook her head. "Investigators tried hard to find some link, a trace. Nothing. I'm sure it's a dead issue, otherwise I would've heard if something had been unearthed. I had a good lawyer, Dee Brown. I'm pretty sure I could've been buried without her. She took another job with a big law firm in D.C., but she keeps her ear to the ground. She'd call if there was news." A burst of laughter caught her attention, and she broke off what she was saying. It was a relief not to continue talking. This need to tell Aaron so many things was unexpected. She looked back at him, wondering at his magic, the pull he had on her.

His smile was hot and sweet. How easy it would be to lose herself in Aaron, to forget her past, herself. He was so warm and caring . . . and so sexy . . . and so wild. There was a sudden, unaccustomed warm dampness between her thighs. The melting, yielding sensation was not new . . . but it had been damned rare in her life. It rocked her that Aaron could call up such a sensual response in her with light banter. Unseeing, she whirled around, heading into the middle of the large room, hoping to lose herself in his family.

For the length of the cocktail hour she was in a pink haze. When she thought of it later in her room, she had to wonder if she'd made any intelligible remarks.

Aaron stayed at her side even during dining. The roaring in her ears kept her from responding to his queries, his concerned smiles.

She was glad when she could retire.

Aaron followed her up the stairs. He touched her arm when she would've entered her room. "What's wrong?"

"Nothing. Your family has been wonderful."

He stared at her for a long moment. "Someday you'll tell me about all your bogeys, Dynasty."

She looked up at him without answering that. "Good night."

He jammed his hands on his hips, his brooding gaze staying on her until she'd closed her door.

Dynasty leaned back against it, closing her eyes. "Good night, Aaron," she whispered, one tear trickling down her cheek. Damn him for getting under her defenses.

The next day dawned bright and warm, soon to be hot. The sun was half a copper plate when Dynasty rose. She showered, then donned jeans, a short-sleeved cotton shirt, and canvas sneaks. Maybe she would find an amenable horse like Stormy and go riding. If not, it would be enough to meander down the lanes and look at the wonderful stock.

Getting downstairs was a pleasant surprise. Instead of using the front stairs, she wandered down the hall and found another staircase she assumed would lead to the back of the house.

Intriguing aromas wafted up to her. The kitchen! She stepped around a curve in the stairs and she was there. A huge airy room already smelling of yeast, tart preserves, and smoky ham.

Seeing tall and wide steel double doors, she opened the refrigerator and found orange juice, a plum, carrot sticks, and some grapes. She took a jar of homemade preserves and spread some on a slice of fresh bread, then sat at the breakfast counter to eat her light but delicious repast. The carrot sticks she wrapped in a paper towel and put in her pocket. She wasn't above bribing a horse.

Outside the air was like new wine, warm but clear enough to make her inhale and exhale in joy.

Eschewing the stable, she walked around the house to the crossword puzzle of white-fenced lanes that intersected pasture and grazing area.

To her delight many of the horses galloped over to see her. She stayed back from the fence, not sure of the protocol with strange horses. "Hi. You are all so handsome."

"They thank you."

Dynasty jumped. "Don't sneak up on people that way."

Aaron moved back, laughing, holding his hands up. "Sorry. Didn't mean to do that. You went up a foot. I thought you'd hear me."

"Well, I didn't." She was inordinately glad to see him. That was one irritant. He looked like a Ralph Lauren model for the great outdoors in jeans, plaid shirt, and work boots. His hair was tousled. Tall, graceful, gentle, and masculine. What a mix. He could be the greatest lure of the twentieth century. "Are you going riding?" she asked.

"Only if you are. I saw you out the window and came after you."

She took a step back. "Has anyone ever told you that you take too many fences, too fast and too soon?"

"No. Though when I was younger I was told I rushed them. Does that help?"

"Nothing does," she murmured.

"I don't understand." He put his hand up, palm outward. "Don't explain. I probably wouldn't like . . ." His focus moved from her face to something beyond her.

"What?" she asked when he frowned.

"I don't know. Stay here."

"No." She followed right behind him. "What is

it?" She tried to look around him. His back was too broad.

"Let me find out first, then—"

"I'm coming."

He glanced over his shoulder. "Stubborn."

"So are you."

He shook his head, then looked forward again. "Damn!" He started to run, then dropped to his knees beside a crumpled form in the lane.

Dynasty went down beside him. "Oh. Poor thing. Your dog?"

Aaron shook his head. "I'd better get him to the clinic. Fast."

"I'll help."

A smile twisted his mouth. "That offer doesn't surprise me, Dynasty." He lifted the dog, ignoring its feeble growls. "By the way, have I told you I like saying your name?"

She was beginning to understand him. He'd say provocative things to spark her temper. Was he distracting her attention from the dog? Or was it more? Aaron Burcell had too many levels to count. Being tied emotionally to him could bring an avalanche of pain, a volcano of anguish, a tidal wave of regret. She shook her head, glad to be walking behind him, quite sure her feelings showed on her face. "It's a good trek back to the house," she said.

"We're not going there. There's a service barn just beyond that paddock. If we're fortunate, one of the trucks will be there. We'll use that."

Dynasty nodded, even though she knew he

couldn't see it. "You seem fated to rescue animals. Related to St. Francis of Assisi, patron saint of animals?"

"Me?" Aaron shook his head. "I don't have the brood you do."

"All happenstance."

Directly ahead was the building he'd described. She followed him through the high, wide doors. When he called out, no one answered him, so he went right to a truck with a rusted-out body and dents along the doors. It had obviously seen better days. "Field truck," he said. "Don't let the outward appearance fool you. This baby is well tuned."

"I know. Everyone in the family can take a car apart and put it back together. What a gaggle of princelings."

"Aren't we?" Aaron grinned at her. His amusement faded when he placed the dog on the truck bed, and it whimpered. "Easy, fella. You'll be fine. Who worked you over? Where do you come from?"

"What if his owner did this?" Dynasty whispered, not realizing she did or why.

"Then he won't get him back. Must be quite a sight when he's in shape, though. Looks to be part Great Pyrenees and a few other bloods." He proffered the keys he'd taken from the wall. "Why don't you drive and—"

"No. You know the truck better than I. You drive."

"We'd better hurry."

They covered the animal with cargo quilting,

then Aaron ran to the driver's side, pulling open the door.

Climbing into the back of the pickup, Dynasty curled her body around the dog, hoping to shelter him from bumps and stinging breezes in the open bed.

The truck started with a muted roar, then spun out of the barn and down the access drive.

The road was rough. Aaron must've taken short-cuts, Dynasty thought. More than once she was glad there was a tailgate locked at their back. A few jounces would've slid her off the end if not for the barrier.

They skidded to a stop in front of white clapboard dwelling, one story with green shutters. The shingle in front proclaimed that L. Ormond, DVM, resided there.

Aaron came round to the tailgate, released it and reached for the quilt-shrouded animal.

Her backside bumped into soreness, Dynasty shinnied off the end.

"Sore?" Aaron asked.

"You could say that." She reached to take the back end of the dog. When he growled, she reared back. "He's spunky."

"He's hurting," Aaron told her. "I'll take him. Run ahead and open the door."

"He won't die, will he?" Dynasty pushed the door wide. Somehow it would be so unfair. Why should any creature die or be disabled because of another, animal or human? Cruelty was so stupid.

"No." Aaron strode into the waiting room.

Dynasty shut the door behind her. The air-conditioning was welcome in the small anteroom. She walked over to the surgery door and banged on it. It was opened by a surprised woman.

"This is an emergency. He needs help now." Dynasty pointed to the dog, which Aaron still held. "I'm not sure how bad he is."

"All right," the woman said. "Let me take a look."

"Are you the vet?"

"I am. Liza Ormond. And you are?"

"Dynasty Jones." She turned around and gestured to Aaron, who brought the animal into the treatment room.

"What happened?" Dr. Ormond asked as she eyed the dog. "Can you hold his head? I have to examine him. It could cause some discomfort."

Dynasty moved close to Aaron, reaching around him to take hold of the dog.

"I can do it. Don't worry, Dynasty."

When she looked into his eyes, her concern lessened. She stepped back while Aaron held the dog and told the doctor what he knew in short sentences.

More than once the dog struggled as the vet examined him. Aaron held him fast, whispering to him.

Dynasty put her hand on the dog's neck, adding her own soothing words.

"Be careful," Aaron warned.

"He won't bite me."

Both the doctor and Aaron gazed at her for a moment.

"It's better than I thought it'd be," Dr. Ormond said, washing her hands. "Despite some deep cuts and bad bruises, a back leg sprain, this dog is not in a terminal condition."

Dynasty exhaled, returning Aaron's smile when he looked at her. "He must have a good constitution."

The doctor nodded. "You were wise to bring him in right away, though. I'll assume he hasn't had his shots and beef them up, plus give him the antibiotics he'll need to fight any infection that might occur." She started gathering the medicines. "This dog needs care for a few weeks. Though he's not a pure bred, he has good lines, and he's strong. I'd guess he has some Great Pyrenees, because of the coat, or maybe Newfoundland. The jaw looks rottweiler." She smiled. "Some mix. Look at the paws. He's large and could get larger. I don't figure he's more than a year old. Because of his mistreatment, whatever it was, he might be hard to handle."

"I think he's gentle," Dynasty said, putting her hand on the dog's head.

"Are you familiar with the big breeds, Miss Jones?"

"I don't think she's too familiar with any animal," Aaron said, leaning back against a cupboard, his arms folded across his chest, a smile whispering over his lips.

"I can get Animal Rescue to handle this," Dr. Ormond said.

"Thanks," Aaron said. "We can handle it."

Dynasty felt a weird catch in her chest when Aaron smiled at the attractive doctor. "When he's better, I can have him shipped North—"

"He can stay at our farm," Aaron interrupted. "No problem." He looked straight at her. "We'll have something to bring you back to us."

Dynasty inhaled a shaky breath. "All right." His eyes had a lavalike heat, burning through every layer of her being. She forgot the dog and the doctor as he continued to gaze at her. He was doing it again, capturing her, turning the key in her life when she wasn't sure if she wanted the closed door to be opened.

"That's settled then," Dr. Ormond said. "You can take him with you. You should watch that one deep cut on his shoulder. The stitches should be fine. If there's any sort of infection, call me. He's undernourished, and he'll need quiet and medication." She cocked her head. "Actually considering his cuts and bruises, he's in remarkable shape. Very strong animal."

Dynasty saw a touch of regret and poignancy on the doctor's face when she looked at Aaron. It made her feel possessive. Ridiculous, she thought.

Aaron whispered to the doctor, then put money on the table.

Dr. Ormond left them in the examining room, explaining she had to get to a farm. A mare was ready to foal, and trouble was expected with the birth.

"Do you know her?" Dynasty asked Aaron. She bit her lip when he smiled at her.

"Not really. My father talks about her. She's good. I knew Doc Smathers, her predecessor."

"Oh." Dynasty ignored the sudden sweep of relief and watched Aaron carefully lift the dog. "I'll pay for half when we—"

"On my terms?"

"On mine," she riposted.

He laughed. "Open the door and let's get out of here."

Instead of putting him in the truck bed, Aaron went around to the passenger door. "You drive. I'll hold him. That way we can keep him more comfortable."

Dynasty nodded, wondering about driving the truck. When it started on the first try, she exhaled. "He'll need licensing and—"

"I know." He grinned at her when she glanced at him. "I'll take you to the county seat. We can get it there."

The ride back didn't take long. She followed Aaron's directions around the stable to the back.

Two workers came out to the truck, puzzled expressions on their faces.

"Aaron? Something up?"

"Rory. Mike. We found a dog. Hurt. We took him to Dr. Ormond. Now he needs care. The vet says he's pretty good, considering. He needs some pampering. I can take him up to the house, or—"

"No problem," dark-haired Rory said. "I've got

an empty stall, all cleaned and ready to go. We'll put down some quilts and get some food."

"We've got some medicine for him too," Dynasty said.

Rory nodded, smiling. "Nothing but the best, Miss Jones. I promise."

When Rory reached for the dog, the creature growled. "Oh, oh, he sounds like an Irishman," Rory said, his own brogue laced with laughter.

"He's had a very rough time."

Rory cocked his head, studying her. "I can see that, Miss Jones. M' father had the touch with animals. Some say I have it, as well. I'll see to him."

"Thank you."

"I thank you for your faith in me."

"I'll thank someone to open this damned door," Aaron said, jerking his head toward the stable. "This dog's heavy."

Rory opened the door for Aaron, leaning toward him. "So the wind's in that quarter, is it?"

"It is," Aaron said through his teeth.

Dynasty eyed Rory, puzzled, when he bent over with laughter.

NINE

Dynasty studied her image in the mirror, pondering Mel Burcell's comments before she'd come up to dress for dinner.

"You must think us rather frivolous, dear." She'd touched Dynasty's cheek. "We're deeper than that. When you've been with us over the years, you'll see our strong side."

Before Dynasty could answer she'd drifted toward the stairs. "Come along, my dear. We should be ready before the guests arrive."

Dynasty sighed, still staring at herself. Had Aaron convinced his family that they had a relationship? She felt hot as she envisioned what such an alliance would entail. Aaron would be a wonderful lover. "Stop that. Get dressed," she commanded her image.

"I am dressed," she muttered. She'd been at Burcell Farms for three days, and tonight was the barbecue to introduce Dynasty to the Burcells' friends and neighbors. They didn't just work hard on Burcell Farms. They played like demons too.

She frowned at her green dress, not because she disliked shimmery silk or the severe cut of the halter gown with its slit front and back allowing for movement. She wore gold half boots. The ensemble was another carryover from her Wall Street days, when she had the money and inclination to own such things. She hadn't worn it once on Honeysuckle Farm.

Inhaling deeply, she gave a sharp nod. "I can handle what comes. Maybe one day the past will be so buried, it will seem as if it happened to someone else." Wishful thinking? Maybe. Somehow it didn't seem outlandish.

Blowing upward to loosen the tendrils of hair that clung to her forehead, she decided she had time to visit the dog she and Aaron had rescued before she joined the party.

She whirled in front of the mirror. "Ready as I'll ever be."

Slinging a gold change purse over her shoulder, fitted with lip gloss, tissue, and a tiny comb, she fastened the half boots and left the bedroom.

Going down the back stairs to the kitchen, she smiled at the staff, calling each one by name, and went out the door. She didn't hear the comments at her back.

"He's set on that one."

"Good. I like her. Tough enough for this family, she is."

"She'd need to be."

Dynasty hurried to the stable, figuring she had no more than fifteen or twenty minutes. In the air-conditioned stable, she paused to orient herself. The angry whinny to her left had her jumping.

"No need to fret," a man said.

"Rory! You startled me."

"I am sorry. That's just Jack over there. Good lines and blood. Too angry and independent to race. M'father rescued him from a second rate stable. He just lives in style. 'Course I have dreams of racing him, but . . ." Rory shrugged.

"He's big, and quite beautiful."

"Strong as an ox and can run all day at top speed. A super horse, some would say. But, I'm blatherin'. Come with me and see your rescued one. He looks better every time I check on him . . . though he's not that fond of me yet."

"He will be."

"Will he, now?"

Dynasty didn't notice his smirk. She was leaning over the low door of the stall where the dog lay. "Hello, Harry. How are you?" One thump of the tail had her grinning. "Did you see that, Rory? He answered me."

"So he did."

❖————————❖

"Tell me about this killing of the thoroughbreds, Rory."

"Well, it's been going on awhile. M'father was killed because he tried to thwart the scoundrels. You may've heard that."

"Yes, I have. I'm sorry."

"So am I. M'father was a grand man, he was. As to the killing of the creatures, greed alone is the spur I think. It's not poor folk doing this. To their shame the culprits have enough of the wherewithal not to stoop to such crimes. It doesn't stop them."

"Is there no way to search them out?"

"Many ways have been tried. They seem to go around, over, and under any deterrent."

Dynasty gave Harry a final pat, then straightened and turned. She caught her breath when she saw Aaron standing beside Rory.

"Hi, beautiful."

"Hi."

"I thought you meant me," Rory said to Aaron.

"Go away. Get dressed. My mother expects you this evening."

Rory groaned. "Why doesn't she believe me when I tell her I hate all that foofaraw? 'Tisn't me."

"Why should she believe you when she doesn't pay any attention to her children?"

"I'm closer than a child to her?" Rory laughed harder when Dynasty chuckled.

The Irishman walked away whistling.

Dynasty smiled at Aaron, then frowned, puzzled by his expression. "What?"

"You look gorgeous. Why are you down here driving Rory nuts? Aren't I enough?"

Her body flushed from the ankles to eyebrows. "You talk like a fool."

"I feel like one too. Put me out of my misery."

"All right." She looked around her.

Aaron groaned. "You're looking for a shotgun, aren't you?"

She smirked. "You bet."

"Our children are going to be awful. I should warn my parents."

"Stop talking like that." She felt a rising desperation. He could make her love him. Losing him would be more devastating than anything that happened to her in New York. Even Wall Street hadn't penetrated her core. Aaron Burcell could do that. He'd already done it.

"Stop thinking about ways to get rid of me, Dynasty Jones." He reached for her and pulled her into his arms, planting his mouth over hers, searching, questing.

She knew he wouldn't force her. The kiss was powerful, yet more gentle than any she'd ever had. He was asking! She wanted it. To hell with worry. That was always there. She needed to grab a little joy. That was the scarce commodity. She felt his shock when she curled her arms around his neck. His body stiffened, then he folded her tighter to his frame.

"Dynasty," he said against her mouth. "I love

your name. Our first daughter will have the same."
Before she could reply, he'd slanted his mouth over
hers, his tongue thrusting.

She met the invasion with her own, the retaliation
making his body shudder. In her life she'd never felt
such potency. He was letting her lead. He was following. It had never occurred to her it could be so sweet.
In all her previous relationships, she'd emphasized
equality. It had seemed right. This was beyond that
. . . a first. Aaron was giving her the lead, the power,
the orchestration . . . with no hesitancy.

She lifted her head, out of breath, dazed but ener-
gized as she'd never been. "The—the party."

He leaned his forehead on hers. "Okay. I'd rather
not." He lifted his palm and laid it along her cheek.
"We've turned a corner, Dynasty. I hope you know
that."

"I do."

He kissed her eyebrow. "Good. There's no going
back for me. I hope you feel the same."

She inhaled, air shuddering through her. "I . . .
I don't know."

"You probably do, but don't want to talk about
it."

She tried to frown at him, but couldn't. She
stepped back, arranging her clothing, glancing at him
and then away.

"You look even more gorgeous."

"No lip gloss."

He shrugged. "You don't need it. Besides it's on
me."

Her chuckle was shaky. "You look good in lip gloss." She took time to repair her own, though her hand was unsteady.

When she was done, he slipped an arm around her waist. "We'll table it. Now we party."

The dog remained behind, looking out the ajar half door that kept him confined in the stall. He felt better. His stomach was almost full. He'd have preferred raw steak to the warm cereal he'd been fed, but he did feel stronger. Maybe going after the woman with the soft hands would be a good idea. There might be raw meat somewhere. Besides she might need him. So might the man. Harry liked his new home, but he hadn't looked around much. Getting to his feet, he stretched, hardly wincing. He'd follow along and see what they were doing.

Aaron kept Dynasty close to his side as they walked around to the back of the house, but a cluster of guests separated them almost immediately.

"Ms. Jones, how are you?"

Dynasty turned to see an older man standing near her, his hand outstretched. "How nice to meet—" she began.

"How lowering, Ms. Jones. You've forgotten me already." He smiled. "I'd looked forward to renewing our acquaintance."

Dynasty blinked, realizing the figure in front of

her was familiar. And he remembered her. Her past had reared its head. "It's Mr. Steelman, isn't it?"

He beamed. "Indeed. How are you? I can't tell you how happy I was to hear you'd be here this weekend. It bowled me over that at last I was going to be able to congratulate you." He took both her hands in his. "Many of us knew you were innocent. When we offered to be character witnesses for you, we weren't accepted."

"How could that be, Mr. Steelman—"

"Cal, please. We're generally on first name basis on the farms around here."

"You have a farm in the area?"

"Yes. Butternut Ridge, about forty miles north. I've known Mel and Doogie for years." His smile slipped. "Unfortunately, now we've banded together like vigilantes, rather than friends."

"The killing of the thoroughbreds?"

His nod was sharp, angry. "Yes. I've lost three. Burcell Farms has lost two that I'm sure of."

"Stormy . . . er, Moonstruck wasn't killed."

His expression lightened. "I just heard about that. Doogie was saying you've grown attached to the horse."

As Dynasty started to reply, she heard a throaty greeting behind her.

"Darling, why haven't you called?"

Dynasty glanced to her right, registering the soignée beauty of the woman greeting Aaron.

"Daisy," Aaron said. "Good to see you. Have you met Dynasty?"

Dynasty turned, holding out her hand. "How—?"

"Is your name really Dynasty? I thought I had the only peculiar name in this area. I'm Daisy Crumbaugh of Peony Lane. My family have been the Burcells' closest neighbor for years."

Dynasty noted how the other woman's arm was around Aaron's waist. "I can see that." There was acid in her voice. When he inclined his head, smiling, she wanted to smack Aaron Burcell right on his dimple.

Daisy chuckled. "Isn't she cute, Cal? Isn't this the gal you knew on Wall Street, the one that . . . Oh, pardon me, I don't want to embarrass you."

"You won't, Ms. Crumbaugh. I was exonerated."
Aaron chuckled.

Cal Steelman squeezed her arm. "Thatta girl, Dynasty. Stick up for yourself."

"I do."

"I do too," Aaron murmured just above her right ear. When she turned, their lips almost met. "Let's get out of here."

"We just got here," she protested as he took her hand and started leading her toward the far side of the house.

"I'll bring you back in time for dinner," he promised.

"That's not—" she struggled to free herself as she saw Aaron's mother wave to them, then give them a puzzled look. "Let go, Aaron. You're embarrassing your parents."

"You'd have to go a long way to do that. Have I

told you about the time my parents had to bail us out of jail?"

"All of you?"

"That only happened once. The girls were usually easier to handle. Noah, Jody, and I were a different story."

"How many times?"

"About six. It was tough. When the males in the family were mellow, the females were wild, and vice versa. Once my mother tried to run away from home. My father found her when she was boarding a bus. Brought her back to us, kicking and screaming."

Reluctant laughter burst from her. "That's not true." His solemn nod made her laugh harder. She'd forgotten to protest his dragging her off, and he quickly ushered her up the steps of a wide wooden porch with swings, chairs, and tables on it.

Aaron stopped next to the railing, leaned down, and kissed her, his lips moving on hers, his tongue entering and taking possession, his arms holding her across the shoulders, around the waist. "Don't pull away," he muttered against her mouth.

"I'm not," she said back, freeing her arms and letting them slide around his waist. "I'm getting comfortable."

"Stay that way." Groaning he took her mouth again, kissing her over and over, as though she were food and he needed her sustenance. "Dynasty . . . Dynasty." His mouth sank to hers once more.

Breathing into his mouth she sought oxygen, then the world exploded and she didn't care if she ever

Get 4 *Loveswept*® Romances *FREE!*

Get 4 Loveswept Romances

FREE!

No Risk. No obligation to purchase. No commitment.

breathed again. Aaron Burcell was her only planet, the only world under her feet. She clung to him.

Hours passed. Or was it days? The earth spun off its axis, creating a new constellation just for them.

"Really!"

Dynasty would've reared back at the woman's shocked exclamation, but Aaron's hold on her was too tight. He released her mouth and turned his head a fraction.

"Yes?"

"I can see why you wanted her down here, Aaron. Sowing your wild oats, are you?"

The brittle laughter accompanying Daisy's comment scratched up Dynasty's spine.

The tall, dark woman beside Daisy said nothing, though her features reflected her animosity.

Aaron looked back at Dynasty. "Sowing wild oats, did you say? Not exactly. I can't say that I won't try to convince Dynasty we should live together before we marry, but I wouldn't call that sowing wild oats. Would you call it that, darling?" He smiled at her, his breathing still a bit ragged. "I won't mislead you. Tell me."

"No . . . no. I wouldn't call . . . it . . . that." Dynasty slowly realized that Daisy and whoever had been with her had left the porch. It took more time than that for her to pull herself together. Little penetrated the pink and purple haze pulsating around her. She didn't have the strength to turn her head and check that she was even still on the porch. She felt aloft, in full flight. "You shouldn't give people false impressions."

"I told the truth." Aaron leaned his forehead on hers. "Every word is a commitment to you."

"I've forsworn commitment."

"I haven't. Wooing you—"

"Sounds archaic."

"Don't interrupt. Wooing you is going to be a backward thing. I'll propose, then we'll do the flowers thing and all the trimmings."

"Foolish."

"I think it's beautiful. We should do something exceptional."

"Off the wall is not exceptional." Why was she discussing such a fruitless pursuit with him? Marry him? Her chest heaved, her breathing all but stopped. Fool's game. "This is so—"

"Just don't shut the door. I've already told my parents I want to marry you, and—"

"What?"

"You heard me. I don't like to keep them in the dark."

"Just me, is that it?"

"My parents are more cooperative than you."

"Thank you."

"You're welcome."

"We should go back to the party."

"Why?" He looked toward the back of the house where Chinese lanterns drooped around a screened enclosure large enough for a series of long tables, several barbecues, and a long bar. "They're not serving the food yet."

"Aaron, I don't—"

"It's quick for you, I know. Just don't tip over the cart. That's all I'm asking."

Forehead knitted, she leaned closer to him, caught the grim twist of his mouth. "This isn't all hearts and flowers, is it?"

"I need to have you in my life. But I also need to protect you."

She caught the harsh inflection in his last words. "Why do I need protection?"

"I don't know. Just call it a gut feeling? I only know I'm not happy with what's going on." When she would've pulled back, he caught her close again, kissing her cheek. "It's just conjecture. I was talking to Rory about this—"

"This?"

"My concerns . . . worries. It's nothing I can put my finger on, just some extraneous stuff that could have a connection . . . maybe."

"You're being evasive."

"I told Rory it bothered me that you had Stormy, that it seemed like a happy turn of events. But if it wasn't that, if someone hid the thoroughbred in the mustang herd for a purpose . . . I don't understand my fear . . . yet. I do know you and Dorothy could be thought to be easy prey—"

"When I phoned Dorothy the day we got here, she told me she'd gotten a strange call." Dynasty told him what her friend had said. "I'm not worried, though, Aaron."

"I know. You think you're tough—"

"I don't think it. I am."

"Great. I love that about you."

Her heart banged against her ribs. She moved closer to him, though she was already pasted to his body. "Go on."

"I called Pepper Lally last night and told him how I felt. He might be moving in with Dorothy in the next few days."

"You called him?" At his nod, she exhaled. "Then you really do have a burr under your saddle."

"I do."

"You don't have anything solid that would back this up?"

"No." He rubbed his hands up and down her arms. "As Rory said, even if all this is fabricated, fashioned in my mind, we have to cover all the bases." His expression turned rock hard. "Nobody is getting to you whether this is all a fantasy or not."

"Thank you. How would you know which it is?"

"Maybe we can smoke out some folks. Who knows? There are ways."

"Are you talking about the thoroughbred scandal?"

"If it's connected to you, I am. If it's not, then I'll lose this gnawing feeling." His mouth twisted. "Doogie says I get it from my mother." He sighed. "Dammit! It has to be nothing. Otherwise it's the damnedest coincidence in the world."

"You have to search for the horse stealers."

He waved his hand as if it were the least of his worries. "We'll keep on trying to catch them . . ." He dropped his mouth to hers. "You're my priority, Dynasty Jones."

"Am I?" She'd tried to put force in her words. They'd come out limp, squeaky.

"Yes."

"Meaning?"

"Rory, my father, my brothers, and I are going to be looking at our friends with a more clinical approach."

She swallowed a gasp. "You think some of your horse breeder friends would be in on this?"

"It'd be hard to swallow. We can't wipe away the fact that some prestigious breeders have already been arrested. It'll be damned hard to prove, and even less palatable." He brushed his hand down her cheek. "We have to protect our stock, ourselves, and especially you. If there's someone making money by killing horses, or kidnapping them to other places, we have to know." He clenched his teeth. "If you're in danger, I want to know. I'll take care of it."

"It's so far-fetched, Aaron." She was more touched than she'd imagined. She felt teary, wimpy . . . yet strong and cherished. The crazy amalgam of emotions was alien to her, but it wasn't unpleasant.

"Maybe not."

"Even if there was a connection—and I don't see it—how would you find it, and why hasn't someone done so before now?" Faith in herself had already been sorely tested. Could she take another hit if Aaron thought she was allied with the culprits? He hadn't said that. It still loomed in her mind.

"Don't," he said. "Your face gives you away, beautiful. You can't think I would tie you to anything heinous. I bared my soul to you, lady. One reason is how I feel, the other is because I trust you." He touched one finger to her cheek. "I'm willing to stand in front of a truck to prove that."

It took her a minute to find her voice. "That would be a bit drastic."

"Not to me. I'd go a long way, maybe even mount a crusade, if you need convincing."

His simple tone, the almost flowery words spoken in a down-to-earth manner practically knocked her off her feet. "Thank you."

"Believe in me, Dynasty."

She choked. "I—I guess I do."

"Good enough. I'll go with that . . . for now."

Her gaze flicked away from him, emotion rising in her throat like a flood. "I think people are finding tables. It must be time to eat." She'd never cared less about food. She needed the mundane action to stabilize her whirling feelings and responses.

His gaze followed hers toward the large enclosure. "Fine. Let's join them." He pressed a kiss to her cheek. "We're not done with this, Dynasty. We have a great deal of talking to do. I have plans. Mind if I run them by you?"

"What if I said no?"

"I'd still try to lay them out if you covered your ears."

She didn't answer. Aaron's warmth toward her, the underlying hardness in him as he spoke about protecting her, was a paradox that needed grappling with, and she would . . . once she got a hold of herself.

For a second she had the shivery sensation she was back in Manhattan and waiting for a verdict that could change her life. Maybe it was Aaron's words. Maybe it was more. Aaron! Head and shoulders over most men, he had a craggy stability that drew her. Why him? What twist of fate had brought him to her? Why hadn't he let her despise him? She could almost hate him for making her love him. He made her crazy.

What if there was something to his suspicions? Why would someone include her in such vicious acts against thoroughbreds? She hadn't owned or been interested in horses until a few months ago. It made no sense. Aaron was on the wrong track. If she hadn't been so angry at herself at how easily she'd trusted him, she might've screamed with anguish at the thought of loving and losing him. It could destroy her. Not again! Not again! This time there might be little chance of recovery. In the midst of the warmth of Kentucky hospitality, she felt a chill wind.

TEN

People milled around in an irregular pattern, heading toward the huge buffet. Most had drinks in their hands. Some had canapes. There was no rush toward the long tables groaning with the elegant and the earthy, an enormous assortment of delicious fare.

Dynasty was separated from Aaron as one of his brothers hailed him, and she drifted over toward Aaron's parents, who were having an animated discussion with someone who resembled Mel.

"Doogie Burcell," she heard the other woman say, "it may interest you to know that I have a working knowledge of the law and business. There's no way in blue hades you can claim a nationwide conspiracy."

"I said international."

"You're exaggerating."

"Amabelle Arbuthnot, you're not facing facts—"

"Doogie, please, we have guests," Mel reminded him.

" 'Course we do. That's why this pain in the neck is here. I wouldn't allow your cousin on the place unless you invited her."

Mel opened her mouth.

Her cousin waved her quiet. "Don't intercede, Mel. We both know Doogie has no manners."

Mel bristled. "I wasn't going to—"

"Doogie, you're wrong about the horses," Amabelle said heatedly. "You impugn some of the finest families in Kentucky—"

"And Texas, Florida, Mexico, and New York, and on and on," Doogie said, squeezing his wife's arm, but not backing down. "Here's something you should know, you silly blue blood. Take off the blinders. You might see it for yourself. There's a huge scam in the thoroughbred world right now. It involves wealthy, poor, and the middle. Crooks on every level. Many brave and beautiful thoroughbreds, and other types of horses, are being destroyed for the money the insurance will bring. You damn well know that Braverman and Sons and Insur-net have shut their doors to most breeders. Don't close your eyes. Take it straight for a change, and stop whitewashing the cruelest high level robbery in a hundred years." His head moved up and down like a jackhammer. "It's criminal this practice of faking the death of a thoroughbred, collecting the money, then selling the creature to an inferior stud farm where they're used, undernourished, then killed. After that they're put into a lime pit—"

"Doogie, you've shocked Amabelle—"

"Someone should."

"This is heinous, and cannot be proved," Amabelle said, her breath coming in shallow gasps. "How would you know about—?"

"Because of Casey O'Donal, the most astute stable man and trainer in the business. He traced one of our studs to such a place. By the time the wheels were in motion, Quillen was dead and quick limed. Casey's testimony allowed us to pursue a civil suit." Doogie's jaw hardened. "I won't let it happen again."

"O'Donal's dead. Some said he had mob connections."

Mel gasped. "You're my cousin, Amabelle, but I won't let you talk that way about Casey. He was a most honorable man, and my dear friend. His son works for us, and he's cut from the same cloth."

Amabelle blinked. "I apologize if I've offended you, cousin, but I can't believe—"

"You never see anything, Amabelle." Doogie stomped off, the women staring after him.

"I don't know how you abide that man, Melly."

"I love him," Mel said, and turned to speak to another guest.

Dynasty decided not to try to join either Mel or Doogie at that point. Instead, she wandered over toward the buffet. The aromas of barbecued fish and meats wafted through the air. She was just thinking that she was hungry and would relish the food when she realized she'd been staring into a dog's eyes. He wagged his tail, then turned his attention to the food.

"Harry! No. I mean, come here, that's a good boy," she said through her teeth. "Come on, be nice. I'll give you some caviar." How had he done it? He'd been in the stall, the door shut. Wasn't it? Lord! "Come, Harry, I'll take you back to your stall and I'll bring canapes."

He wagged his tail again, but stayed where he was, his attention caught by enticing aromas.

"How did you get out?" The whisper had hardly left her throat when the dog moved to the main table, laden with assorted viands and fish, the center of which was a huge tray of smoking ribs. "Noooo!" Dynasty saw Aaron turn toward her as she raced for the dog.

"Damn! How the hell did that happen?"

No one answered Aaron's shout.

Harry saw Dynasty coming for him and nimbly leaped onto the first table. A caterer yelled. Shrimp, hot and spicy, slid back and forth on a tray, shooting off into the crowd. Several women screamed. The dog took umbrage and trotted to the far end of the table. The table tipped. Harry managed to intercept several ribs sliding his way, crunching down to hold them in place as he hopped along the length of the buffet. Carvings of gelatin and ice swung and swayed, then caved in and slid under his paws. Various sauces became airborne. Breads of all sorts did somersaults. Meat jounced and jogged along the table, Harry in hot pursuit.

Aaron leaped and missed. "Damn!"

His father turned in time to see the punch bowl waver and dip, its contents becoming a miniature red tidal wave. "I'll be a stud's pup! Look at that dog. Balance and eat. Like a damned high-wire act."

"Doogie!" Mel shouted, her hand going to her mouth.

"I'm on it, darlin'." Laughter burst from him as Aaron made another grab for the dog.

Noah streaked after his father. "Better get the dog, Doogie, Mom's face is getting red."

"I'm tryin', boy." Doogie grabbed the punch bowl. Noah managed to grab the rib tray before it landed on the ground.

"Oh, glory!" Dynasty muttered. "Harry, come to Dynasty. There's a good boy." She bent down, edging closer to where Harry had leaped from the table to the ground. "Stay still."

"Is this the dog you rescued?" Clare spoke in a whisper, as though she feared to spook the dog who was warily eyeing the many humans facing him.

"Yes. Damn his eyes."

"You sure are a fun guest."

"This is not funny." Dynasty closed her eyes for a moment, then lunged for the dog. She missed.

Harry hotfooted it under the table. Dynasty went around, giving chase, vowing to panfry him when she got him. "Come on, Harry. Stop!"

"My money's on Dynasty," Terry drawled, drawing laughter from those near her.

Her husband reached for his wallet. "You're on. Fifty on the canine."

"I'll take a piece of that." Noah slid up next to them. "Hold the ribs for me. Clare! Are you in?"

"Of course. My money's on Dynasty."

"She hasn't got a prayer," Jody interjected, leaping for a basket of breads. "That dog's fast."

In minutes the Burcells had a lottery on the three contestants. Harry. Dynasty. Aaron.

"I suppose I should bet on Aaron. He is my son, after all."

"Mel, you should be ashamed to admit it. And that awful Northerner—"

"Better not bad-mouth Dynasty, Aunt Amabelle," Clare admonished. "Aaron means to have her."

"This family is insane. Put me down for the dog."

"They're out of sight," someone called. "Can anyone see who's in the lead?"

"This isn't Churchill Downs, Howard," a dry voice answered. "It's business as usual at the Burcells. A circus."

Dynasty was out of breath. The dog had stopped to eat the caviar he'd managed to stuff into his very full mouth.

"Gotcha!" Dynasty made a dive, grabbing him by the scruff.

He looked up at her, swallowed, and burped.

"Hold him," Aaron said behind her.

"I don't need help. Don't touch him. I'm going to kill him."

Aaron took deep breaths, then laughed. "Your

face is red, and I think you have barbecue sauce on your lovely dress."

"I don't care. Give me a knife. Stop chewing," she said to the dog. "Everyone watched you, you fool. People won't eat because of you."

"Sure they will," Aaron said, putting his arm around her and leaning down to pat the dog's head.

"Don't touch that Benedict Arnold. After all we've done, he pulls a stunt like this."

"Ribs are a great inducement," Aaron murmured, kissing her hair.

"He was eating caviar too."

"Very refined taste for a mixed breed."

"He's a miserable hound."

"The vet said nothing about that."

"You know what I mean."

"Yeah, but I'm having the best time I've had in hours because of him. How can I be mad at him?" He leaned down and kissed her mouth. "Ummm, you taste good. Ribs?"

"Canapes," she said through her teeth.

The dog looked up, inclining his head, looking as though the bubbled mustache and beard of Beluga caviar was an ordinary addition to his face. His big tongue took care of that.

"Of all the—" Dynasty was interrupted by Aaron's kiss, melting her to her instep.

Harry eyed the man and woman as they swayed back and forth as though they'd been tied together.

He weighed his chances. His paws dripped red stuff that had come from a big round dish. It didn't taste bad. He'd liked the ribs and the bubbly fish. Better than kibble. Licking his chops, he wondered if he should run again. He contemplated the two clamped together. They'd been good to him. He felt stronger each day. The food was good, especially all those different things on that long table. Hunkering down to his belly, he decided. He might get whupped for taking the food. People got excited about things like that. Better take a couple of licks and stick with the two who were glued together. They were his best option. Harry sighed, putting his head on his outstretched paws.

"Harry," Dynasty gasped, wrenching back from Aaron. Panting, she pointed downward. "We've got to make him mind."

Aaron kissed her cheek, her nose, her eyebrows. "Atta girl," he muttered. "Make him toe the line. Look how quickly you brought me to heel."

Amusement bubbled up in her. "Shush," she managed. "Look. He seems to be sorry."

"Bull. He's planning how he can get back to the buffet." Aaron looked down at the amiable animal. "There's not even a bit of caviar left on his muzzle. He's neat. I'll say that for him."

Dynasty winced. "Come along, Harry. You, too, Aaron. We have to face the music."

"We? You didn't jump on the buffet. Neither did I. I refuse to take the fall for this manic thief of a canine. He had a nice stable. His own stall. It was warm. He was well fed. None of the rest of the guests did aerobics in the food. He can face my mother alone."

"That's not funny."

"I'm not being funny. I was one of six children. We learned fast not to involve ourselves if we were innocent." He looked over his shoulder. "Let's make a break for it. We'll get to the airport, grab a flight to Chicago, and—"

"Were you ever innocent?"

"That's beside the point. I'm not taking the blame. Harry faces my mother by himself."

Dynasty shook her head. "Come along . . . Harry."

The dog stood and trotted after her.

"Hey!" Aaron called. "Wait. I want to see this. Well, I don't . . . but I suppose I'm in it." Aaron moved to her left, slipping his arm around her waist. "This is crazy. Why don't we elope to Las Vegas?"

"Don't you think your folks have had enough upset for one day?"

"They're tough. No problem."

"You're a sadist. Your mother will ask me to leave."

"Better yet, we'll beat her to it and leave ourselves."

Dynasty scowled at him. "Don't you care that she'll be furious, that she'll throw me off the place?"

"She won't. She knows you're going to be her daughter-in-law. She'll bless you for taking me off her hands."

"You're crazy."

"Nope. My mother will be happy to welcome you to the family. She's been trying to foist me off on anyone under eighty for years. She'll be turning cartwheels when you take me to Honeysuckle Farm and keep me there."

"That's crazy."

Aaron frowned. "She's not crazy. She's desperate. Help her out."

"You're crazy."

"About you."

"Stop. We have to talk to your mother."

"Why are you glaring at me? I didn't get into the caviar."

They rounded the corner of the house. A hundred faces turned their way.

"Oh, Lord," Dynasty whispered.

"Hi, everybody," Aaron called. "Got the culprit."

"Who got who? We have wagers here. Big money," Noah said, waving a wad in the air.

"Lord!" Dynasty couldn't look at the Burcells.

"I think the dog stopped, finished what he had, then let Dynasty grab him."

There were groans and shouts of glee. Money was passed out.

Clare approached, looking pained. "Dynasty, you could've tried harder. I lost fifty bucks on you."

"Ah . . . sorry."

"You should be." Clare patted her shoulder. "Better luck next time."

"Never again, if I can help it," Dynasty muttered. Only the caterers didn't look up, busy as they were setting up more refreshments after cleaning away the disaster caused by Harry.

Taking a deep breath, Dynasty approached her hostess, Harry at her side.

"Mrs. Burcell . . ." Dynasty began.

Mel waved a hand. "My dear, don't think I hold a grudge because you lost." A wrinkle appeared between her eyebrows. "Though I thought you more fleet-footed than that."

"Mrs. Burcell, I—"

Mel patted her hand. "Not that I don't think you were quite brave to go after the creature, though he does seem more subdued." She patted Harry's head.

"He wants to check out the new load of chow being set up," Aaron said.

For the first time the caterers looked up . . . and glared.

"No, he doesn't," Dynasty said, pinching Aaron.

"Oww, you're arousing me, darling."

Dynasty's mouth dropped.

"Behave yourself, Aaron," his mother said, her smile in place. She took Dynasty's arm. "My dear, it was perfect. A diversion was just what we needed. My cousin was about to kill my husband. I wasn't sure just how to stop her."

Dynasty felt weak. She shook her head, helpless humor turning her knees to jelly. "You're just being so good about this. I can't tell you how sorry I am. I should've checked to make sure he was confined."

"Nonsense, my dear. I'm sure it was Aaron's fault."

"I knew it," Clare said, pointing at her brother.

Aaron shook his head. "No way was this my doing."

"It was, I'm sure of it," Terry said.

Mel nodded. "He was always creating a disturbance."

Aaron frowned at Dynasty. "I told you we should've cut out of here. I'm getting blamed. Damn you, Harry, stand up like a man and admit you were alone in this."

Mel patted the big head near her leg. "He does seem very sweet."

"Get a hammer and smash him, Melly," Amabelle said. "Look at my gown. Stained with that awful rib juice."

Mel stiffened. "It isn't awful. They used my very own recipe and everyone loves it—"

"I don't care. Look at me. This was a Hartnell original."

"I can't kill him, Amabelle. He belongs to Dynasty, and she dotes on him."

Dynasty tried to smile at Aaron's scowling aunt.

"I think you should kiss the dog, Aunt Amabelle. I haven't had so much fun in . . ." Noah's voice died at his mother's look.

"What a party, Mother. You are definitely hostess of the year."

"Thank you, Jody."

The dry note in Mel's voice had Dynasty wincing as she bent over Harry. "I should kill you myself," she muttered, stroking the animal, whose clear-eyed stare never wavered from her.

"He's an asset to my father. He finds these parties very dull," Aaron said, leaning close to her. He grimaced when the dog licked his face. "Get away, hound. I want somebody else's kisses."

"I think I should leave. I'm going to pack."

"Nonsense, Dynasty, m'dear. Most fun I've had in days," Doogie said, putting his arm around her waist. When the dog growled, he laughed. "Harry is as possessive as Aaron. Are you taking him back with you to New York? I'd sure like to keep him here."

Dynasty raised her head, her smile twisted. "He might not last another day here." She looked around, her smile dying. Despite the hurried efforts of the caterers, there was still a good bit of debris. "Good Lord. It's like a tornado. I'm so sorry."

Doogie frowned. "How's that? You didn't do anything."

"Harry followed me."

Doogie shrugged. "I think he followed the smells." He glanced at the army of caterers cleaning up. "Made a good choice. Fish is good for a canine. Can't abide that caviar stuff myself. Always feel like I'm eating soft buckshot." He shook his head. "Awful."

"Don't say that," Mel cautioned. "Dynasty, are you worried about your beautiful dress, dear? Don't. Terry has already steered some of the ladies to our bedrooms. Noah, for his sins, will take care of the men. Ample clothes, ample stores. No problem."

Dynasty stared at the diminutive woman, her mouth opening and closing. She swallowed once, twice. Then the pent-up tears, that could always be controlled and dammed, that had not escaped once during her hearing and trial, slipped down her face, one after another until there was a torrent.

"Oh, child, don't," Mel said, her voice breaking. "Doogie . . . ?"

"Dynasty, child, don't." Doogie reached out his arms.

Aaron stepped around him. "I'll take her to her room. She needs sleep. I think I'll call it quits too. All right, Mother?"

Mel nodded, her eyes worried as she watched them walk away, Aaron's arm tight around Dynasty. "He could be hurt, my love. He's like you. Loves too hard."

Doogie scooped her close to him and kissed her. "Never regretted loving you like that." He frowned. "In a way I hope they don't have children. That's what hurt me the most about loving you. Seeing you in pain."

"Don't be foolish. You loved the children."

"I'd rather adopt."

"Too late."

They laughed together.

Mel looked over her shoulder at her son. "He could be so hurt . . . so crushed if she can't love him." Sighing she put her arm around her husband's waist.

ELEVEN

Dynasty sat in her room staring at the door long after Aaron had left. She knew he'd wanted to stay with her. He'd kissed her twice. There'd been buckets of heat in them, a questing for more. She'd wanted him just as much. Maybe he'd seen that in her, as she had in him. She sighed. Too long aloof from the many pleasures that could occur between a man and a woman, she'd let caution rule her. Aaron's smile had been gentle, not condemnatory. He hadn't pushed, not even suggested. Damn him.

"Fool!" she said aloud. "You could be alone for the rest of your life . . . and not be protected. He's already over your barricade." She shrugged, not sure whether she was winning or losing the argument with herself. "So? It's not permanent. What is? You learned not to whimper. Now stop running. Take a chance. What can you lose?" Her mind answered. Just all the peace on the planet, and gain instead a lifetime of regret, hurt that couldn't be brushed away or aside. "You can have that anyway . . . and along with the regret will be a big wish that you'd had him once, that he'd had you."

She argued with herself, all the while she undressed. She stared at her jeans long and hard before she pulled them on, then slid into a cotton shirt, tugging it down over bared shoulders and breasts. When she was tying her sneakers, pros and cons rivered through her brain.

Standing, she exhaled. "We, who are about to die, salute you," she muttered. "Great time to think of Suetonius. All those damned long nights of studying Latin because it would help with business and finance, and what do I remember?"

Aaron wasn't staying in the main house that night, as he'd done since her arrival. He'd told her he was going back to his own place, on the grounds. It seemed each of the Burcell children had separate dwellings, when and if they cared to use them. Aaron was at his.

Down the back stairs she went. Quiet, she entered the kitchen, wondering what excuse she could give for going out late at night, dressed for barn chores, while there were guests. To her relief none of the kitchen staff or caterers spared her a glance. She went out the rear door, prepared to fumble her way in the dark. Not so. The well-lit stable area, the tall barn lights outlined her path. She hadn't been to Aaron's place, but she'd been told where it was.

There were still guests aplenty. Sounds of the

party faded as she moved deeper into the land behind the house. The numerous barns were black silhouettes against a midnight-blue sky, dotted with firefly stars. The corkscrew path was lined with a fragrant border. In the false light she couldn't tell if the tiny blooms were white or yellow. She inhaled and tried to pretend she wasn't nervous.

The night noises of summer in Kentucky were as loud and myriad as they were in Yokapa County. It was hot, but not steamy. She was overwarm, not because of the temperature, but because of the risk she was taking. A great deal swung on what she was doing.

She moved quickly on the well-lit walkways. She saw no one. It crossed her mind that Aaron might not be home. Perhaps he had decided to go back to the party, spend more time with Daisy of Peony Lane. She didn't stop. She rounded a hedge, black in the shadows, and there it was, at least she assumed it was Aaron's place.

She dabbed at the perspiration on her upper lip with one finger.

Dynasty looked down at herself. She wasn't exactly clad for a seduction. "Then I'll tell him what I'm here for." The sound of her whispers sent her to the shallow porch of the good-size brick house. She was about to rap on the door, but when she touched the handle, it turned. She figured she'd find him staring at her when she opened it. She pushed the door wide. Nothing. He was gone . . . though he'd left one lamp lit. Then she heard singing and smiled. Relief was a spur that sent her up the wide floating stairway of the very modern interior. At the landing she looked at three doors, opened the middle one, turned left at the sound of the slightly off-key voice imitating Vince Gill.

Moving to another door, she opened it. Inside the spacious, steamy bathroom, she made another decision and stripped off her clothes.

Naked, she stared at Aaron's outline in the shower stall. It was a large one. The door would open toward her. She reached, pulled it open, and stepped in next to him, even as his head was turning. No doubt he'd felt the draft.

"Hello," she said. "I don't mean to intrude . . ." She stopped when he reached out, started to speak, and slipped. His hands went wide, then his feet. He thudded against the tile wall, then fell in a heap at her feet. "I guess I should've called."

Aaron gazed up at her, all the way up, then down, then up again. "No need," he said, his voice hoarse. "Glad to have you. That is, good to take a shower . . . not that you need one. I don't like to shower alone . . . not that I don't usually. Damn!"

"Thank you. I think I understand." She reached down a hand. "Let me help you."

"I guess you'd better. I . . . ah . . . you're not . . . a . . . Are you real?"

She pinched her waist with her free hand. "I think I am."

"Don't let me die now," Aaron muttered to some deity.

"Did you plan on it?"

"No, but my breathing's in trouble, and my heart beat's at a danger level. I'd sure like to hold you before I pass out."

"Good idea."

"Thanks." He scrambled upright, his hands lifting, then falling back to his sides. "I'm naked."

She bit her lip to keep from laughing. Had she ever felt so relaxed? "I know. People are like that when they shower."

"I don't want to scare you off."

"You would if you had an overcoat on."

He smiled, steamy water plastering the hair down on his head. He reached for her waist and pulled her under the water. "Did you walk down here like that?"

"Sure. I generally walk around other people's property unclothed."

"Poor joke."

"Of course I didn't, so stop scowling."

"Sorry. I was imagining someone else seeing this."

"No one did."

He beamed at her. "Good." He leaned down and kissed her lightly. "I can't believe you're here."

"Neither can I." His arrested look had her puzzled. "What?"

"Don't think I'd coerce you to stay, though I hope like hell you won't leave me." His hands feathered over her breasts and hips, skimmed across her thighs.

Air caught in her lungs. Blood backed up in her veins. She stared at him.

"What're you thinking?" he asked. "Have I turned into a werewolf? I know there's been some changes . . . besides the one in you. Tell me what's on your mind."

Dynasty exhaled. "Just wondering how many times you've done this." Why had she said that? It hadn't been on the front of her brain. His body had. How muscular it was, the flat planes of his stomach, the taut response to her own excitement. All words were foolish. Nothing but marbles tossed in the hubcap of a speeding car.

Aaron leaned back, a slow smile lighting up his face. "Well, I like that you wonder. It makes me think you could be—"

"Don't say it. I hate that word. It has no part in my life."

"No envy, either."

"Only about depth of compassion and talent. I admire painters, writers, and musicians. I might not be exactly envious. I'd like to be able to do it." The long drawn-out explanation of nothing! She was prattling. Stop!

"And you're devoid of talent? I don't think so, business lady, berry entrepreneur." He took a deep breath. "I realize we're putting off the discussion of making love—"

"Is that what happens with you? Discourse?"

"Not exactly. This is all new to me, pretty lady." He kneaded the flesh at her waist. "You're so soft and beautiful . . . yet strong and sweet." He frowned. "Wait. I didn't finish my thought. You're very distracting. Remind me not to take you to the office—"

"Do you have one?"

"No. Well, yes, I do. In Manhattan and here on the farm. Downstairs in—Stop that! I want to finish. You implied you had nothing—"

"Did not."

"Shhh. None of that is true . . . about you having nothing."

Warm water continued to pulse around them as Aaron began to wash her with a long, soft loofah sponge. "It doesn't matter," she said, her eyes drooping closed.

"It does. A genius for marketing, prophesying when to buy and sell is certainly an art form . . . isn't it?"

Mirth and more trembled on her lips and faded back. "Perhaps I once thought it was. It might not be so important now."

"It's vital that you see how I value you, Dynasty. Not just as an incredible woman, filled with accomplishments, but a person with great compassion, a capacity to keep learning that I haven't often come across, personally or in business." He kissed her cheek. "It's not unusual to be in awe of what others do. Just don't forget how wonderful you are."

"I've never been this philosophical in a shower."

"From now on all our showers will have intellectual stimuli."

She studied him. "I can see you're an expert at stimulation."

"Yeah. You're my greatest stimulation."

"I'm glad I came."

He leaned down and kissed one nipple, inhaling sharply when she gasped. "So am I."

She lifted her hand to his face. "I decided to give in to . . . want."

"I can go along with that. I've never been so aroused. I have to hope my mind won't blow and my body follow. That'd be embarrassing."

Feeling both flustered and serene, she stroked his face. "This could be a one-night stand. Have you thought of that?"

"My imagination has taken me further." His grin faded. He blinked. "Is—is this it? We're going to have sex."

"I think so. Don't look so surprised."

"Stunned is a better word." He leaned over her. "Is it within the game rules to tell you I love you?"

"Are there rules?"

"From what I hear, long lasting ones . . . if the right conditions apply."

"And they are?"

"Say yes to everything. I love you."

"I've never found those words to have much weight."

"Oh? Then we'll put them aside for now. Would you like to see the rest of my place? Like my bedroom?"

She smiled. "Not here?"

"No! It's going to be right between us, not some rushed coupling in a shower." He turned off the spigot.

She reached for a towel.

His hand was there before her, and he patted her skin dry, pausing to kiss her in all the special places. He swiped at himself with the same towel, then he lifted her high into his arms. "I can't believe you're here."

"Neither can I."

"Don't back away. I want you with me."

She curled her arms around his neck. "Good plan."

The bedroom was large with one wall a semicircle of glass and wood.

"Tell me about your house."

He sighed. "We certainly are putting things off. Fortunately I have a good imagination . . . and staying power." He sat down on the bed, cuddling her on his lap. "What would you like to know?"

"Everything."

"Of course. Comfortable?"

"Well . . . your lap . . . There is a slight . . . impediment." Laughter bubbled in her when he flinched.

"That's me. And it isn't funny. You arouse me, ma'am. Can't help it." He kissed the corner of her mouth, then tightened his hold, putting his mouth to her ear." About the house. All the Burcells have their own place with three to four acres around it. Mine is an old brick place they would've called a dowry house in old England. This was a mother-in-law abode in Kit Carson's day. Of course we've added a few amenities . . . like indoor plumbing, central heating, all the good stuff."

"Happy to hear that." She experimented with her own exploration. Though her experiences with men weren't extensive, she'd been very taken with one or two. Never had she felt the sexual curiosity Aaron stirred in her. Her finger ran up and down his cheek, coursing his neck.

"If you want any more information . . . tell me now."

"Your voice is hoarse again," she told him.

"You're killing me, Dynasty Jones."

She grinned. His answering smile pulled at her as nothing else ever had. He had a power, as if he'd thrown a net over her. Paradoxically, the tighter he pulled it, the freer she felt.

"Dynasty," he murmured, bending toward her. "It's been a long one."

"What?"

"The search. I didn't think I was even on one until I met you. Then I realized how fatigued I was."

"This conversation could be considered gibberish."

"No doubt. I hope you understand it."

To her great cost she did. Nothing worthwhile came without a price. She'd learned that on the Street. Leaning forward, she kissed his cheek. "I'll give you no promises."

"I'll keep asking."

She cupped his jaw with her hands. "I learned the hard way not to trust lovers."

"I'll be your friend . . . and your lover, my love." His hands clasped her waist. "I would like to be that to you."

She swallowed. "Tall order."

"I'm equal to it."

She took a deep breath and stood up, bringing him with her. "I might've ruined it. I'm supposed to be drenched in perfume and dripping in silk."

"I think you're so beautiful . . . in rags or nude, you're special." He lifted her hand. "I feel privileged to look at you."

She gasped at the unexpected gallantry. Confused, she looked down at the silk coverlet, edged with hand-embroidered lace. "We should remove this."

"We won't. We'll get under it."

She felt as though he led her through a courtship ritual as he helped her under the covers and followed her.

As he folded her into his arms, the phone rang.

"Damn! I should've taken it off the hook." He glared at Dynasty. "I'm not answering. The machine will get it."

"Fine." Dynasty caressed his cheek, feeling the heat of his body so close to hers, reveling in it.

His answering machine turned on, and they heard Doogie's voice. "Aaron, pick up. They found Maxima in the ravine behind the west pasture. Doesn't look like she had the fall by herself. Both her front legs were broken. We had to shoot her."

Dynasty heard the sob in Aaron's father's voice. "Pick it up, Aaron. We'll have another time."

He kissed her hard and picked up the phone. "Dad, I'm on my way. Did you call the police?"

Dynasty watched Aaron nod, then he was sliding out of bed. She was right behind him.

He looked over his shoulder. "Stay."

She shook her head. "I'm going with you. I want to help."

His smile was bitter. "I don't think there's much we can do, but let's go."

They dressed together, barely looking at each other, lost in thought.

Aaron preceded her down the stairs. At the bottom he turned, his hands outstretched. "Don't forget I love you, Dynasty."

Her heart jerked at the words. It was as though he'd sounded a death knell. She didn't consider herself overly superstitious. At that moment, though, she would've given anything for him to call back the words. It was as though in tying himself to her, he'd endangered himself.

"What is it?" he asked.

"Nothing. Something walked on my grave."

"Ahh, the old Gaelic superstitions. You mustn't proclaim love too loudly or the demons will pick it up and smite you."

"Yes, that must be it." She tried to smile. Her face had frozen with a deep icy fear. "Aaron . . . maybe we shouldn't go down where the horse is."

"Are you upset? That's all right. You stay here, love. I'll be right back."

"No! I mean . . . I've got to go with you." She passed him, knowing he was watching her, puzzled. How could she tell him that her nervous reaction meant nothing when to her it did. She'd protect him, somehow.

They got into Aaron's truck, which was almost as battered as the one they'd used to take Harry to the vet.

"I should go home soon," she said tentatively.

He glanced at her before looking back at the rutty track they traversed in the dark. "I'll go with you."

Surprised, she looked at him. "Why?"

His mouth twisted. "You don't need me to answer that. You damn well know how you make me feel."

Suffused with heat, she welcomed the dimness of the truck's interior. "Your work is here, your home . . ."

The long pause was unsettling. "I admit we have a great deal to settle between us, but one thing I'm solid on, lady, is how I feel about you. It happened fast, but it hasn't changed, except to deepen." He swallowed. "It's going to be this way a long time."

"I'm . . . I fear commitment. A hangover, I admit, but it's there."

"We can work on that, if you're willing."

She smiled. "How do you get rid of bogeys?"

His right hand reached for hers, bringing it to his mouth. Then he released it to grab the vibrating wheel. "It takes time. I'm willing to invest in us. How about you?"

She exhaled. "It's worth a shot."

"Yeah." He wheeled around a sharp bend and crossed an overgrown pasture. "There. Up ahead. Where the lights are." He drove across the field at teeth-jarring speed, then stood on the brakes. "This isn't pretty. Why don't you stay here?"

"What will you look for?"

"The why, the how." He ground his teeth. "Then the who." He leaned over and kissed her. "Here's a flashlight in case you follow me. Don't worry about strangers. You're on Burcell land, and there'll be a good number of our people all around you. No one will hurt you here." He hopped out of the truck.

Dynasty watched the wavering beam of his flashlight as he joined a group of men near a clump of trees.

She studied the group for a time, then leaned her head back and listened to the night noises. It was almost autumn. Where had the time gone? She'd met Aaron in August. It seemed years ago, not mere weeks.

Not wanting to dwell on how she'd come to depend on the man, how he seemed such a large part of her life, she opened her door, grasped the flashlight, and jumped to the ground. She pressed the door closed, so no noise would disturb the wide circle of men, seeming intent on the ground. What did they hope to find?

Shining her light on the ground, she studied the

area, wondering what the men would discover. Moving slowly, her flashlight waving in front of her, she wasn't sure she'd know if she came on anything worthwhile.

A sparkle in the high grass caught her eye. Leaning down to look, she couldn't quite make it out. A shell casing? She was lifting it when another sheen near it caught her attention. She picked it up, feeling a surge of familiarity, yet as she stared at the funny corkscrew-shaped key ring, she couldn't put it together. The more she looked at it, the grayer was the thought. It escaped her.

"Found something?"

She looked up, startled. A man stood over her, his face dimly illuminated by the flashlight he held. "Oh! Mr. Steelman! You scared me."

"I'm sorry. I thought you saw me. Do you have anything I should show to Doogie?"

"Maybe. I don't think it's anything." She handed him the key ring.

He took it from her, turning it in his hand. "I agree. I don't think it's anything. I'll give it to Doogie. It could belong to him."

Dynasty nodded, watching him walk away. It wasn't until he'd joined the others and she put her hand in her pocket that she remembered the shell casing. Oh well, she could give it to Aaron. Still walking around, she looked closer, moved slowly, figuring that even a small article like a key ring might be beneficial to the Burcells. Was there a chance they'd catch the culprits?

At the sudden flurry of activity and shouting, she turned to watch them winch the horse's body up from the ravine. Sickened at the thought, even though her vision was impaired by the cluster of people and bad lighting, she lost her taste for further hunting and went back to the truck. She kept her head down when the trailer carrying the horse passed.

"Are you all right?" Aaron opened the passenger door of the truck and put his arms around her. "You shouldn't have come with me."

"I wanted to, really." She leaned against him. "It's so violent and so unnecessary . . . to hurt the animals." She turned her face into his shirt. "I shouldn't wonder at it. Look what so-called humans do to babies . . . children . . . women."

Aaron kissed her hair. "It's a world that needs more compassion. It needs you, Dynasty Jones." His mouth slid to hers. "So do I. Can I take you back to my place?"

She nodded.

He kissed her, his mouth slanting over hers, his tongue questing at hers.

Happy to be held, letting his passion erase the thoughts of the dead horse, she closed her eyes, clutching him.

"Dynasty," he murmured, drawing out the syllables of her name.

Contentment, excitement, desire, were a wild mix in her as the kiss deepened.

"I guess I can count on you to take care of Dynasty," Doogie said behind Aaron.

Aaron lifted his head a fraction, not releasing Dynasty. "Bet on it."

"I like weddings," Doogie said, walking away. " 'Nite, Dynasty."

"Ah . . . good night, sir."

"I like that girl, Rory," they heard Doogie say to the younger man. "Purty thing, and sweet too."

"I believe you've the right of it, Doogie."

Their voices faded.

Dynasty looked at Aaron. "We're the talk of Burcell Farms."

Aaron shook his head. "We will be when we get married."

"You're still rushing your fences."

"Can't help it." He gave her one more hard kiss, then released her, closed her door, and walked around the front of the truck to the driver's side. "Let's go home, lady."

"Let's." She knew how torn up he was about the horse, but he'd said nothing. "I'm a good listener, Aaron."

He took a deep breath, keeping his eyes on the rough ground they traveled over. "It was a mare, Maxima. She raced against some great thoroughbreds and won her share. She belonged to Cal Steelman primarily, but we'd taken her for a brood mare because her stock is so fine. Great bloodlines. She's produced some fine colts." He shook his head. "I don't get it. She had some insurance on her, not a great deal, and it was made out to my father, who would never kill a horse. I don't get it." He shook his head.

Dynasty squeezed his arm, then rested her hand on her thigh. She felt the small lump in her jean's pocket. "Oh. I found a shell casing on the ground—"

"What?"

The truck skidded to a stop, jerking both of them against their seat belts.

Dynasty held out her hand. "I wasn't sure it would mean anything."

Aaron turned the casing in his hands. "Maybe not. It's a common type." He ground his teeth. "We don't shoot much on this farm. This is a precision kind used for hunting large game."

It was as though he were talking to himself. Dynasty sensed his agitation. "It hurt to lose the horse."

He nodded. "Yeah. She is . . . was special." He shrugged. "To us they're an extended family, stupid as that may seem."

"It doesn't sound that way to me."

He tucked the shell casing in the pocket of his jeans. "That's because you're a very loving woman, Dynasty Jones." He leaned across the gear shift, stopping an inch from her lips.

Knowing the choice was hers, she closed the gap, giving him access to her mouth. She was almost used to the avalanche of heat that rolled over her. When he pulled back, she felt bereft, as if he'd taken part of her with him.

Aaron drove like a madman the rest of the way home.

TWELVE

His house looked small to him for the first time. Always it had seemed just right, the old brick's rough surface having the patina of age that pleased him. He'd had the trim painted cream, the doors, front and back, turquoise. The high, full moon was almost like daylight, softening the colors, enhancing the handmade brick. He parked the truck in front, not bothering to take it around the back, more than half sure Dynasty would insist on returning to the main house.

He faced her. "Home again." His whisper seemed to disturb her concentration. She was looking at his house, as though she was seeing it for the first time.

"It's more than lovely," she murmured. "You've allowed its soul to preen."

Taken aback by her words, he stared at his domicile. "I like seeing it through your eyes. It belonged to my great-great-grandmother first. The women in the family called her a termagant, so the tale goes. There's a small painting of her inside. She's ramrod straight, her chin is up, and she looks tough enough to have lived as long as she did in her time. Eighty years." His grin twisted. "My mother says I get my hardheadedness from her."

"Strange. I thought it was pure concrete."

He grinned at her. Then he got out of the truck, went around to her side, and opened the door. "Oh, you did." Aaron lifted her out, sweeping her up into his arms and around in a circle. "You're like a little girl. Your smile. The light in your eyes—"

"I'm no girl," Dynasty said, her tone taut, though she felt giddy and childish, held as she was. Heat flared in Aaron's gaze, lighting her fire at the same time. He was too powerful a man, but now was the moment she wanted, that she would cherish, no matter what the future held. He was letting her slip down his body, her shirt gathering and creeping upward with every downward motion. "This isn't real," she whispered, not sure if it was for him or her.

"I'd debate it with you, but I'd rather concentrate elsewhere."

"So would I." His beaming smile almost undid her. She was glad he still held her.

When he swept his arm under her knees and cuddled her close, she looked at him in surprise. "Now what? You just put me down a second ago."

"True. This is to impress the grand old lady who inhabited the place once. I'm sure she's around somewhere. I'm being traditional," he said, walking to the door. "Carrying you across the threshold. Symbolic to me. Nothing to you."

"Don't be cute," she said.

"You're the cute one," he told her, his mouth moving down onto hers. When he lifted his head, he groaned.

"Too heavy?" she asked.

"Too sexy," he said, his breath coming harder.

She laughed, surprising herself. The long lost confidence she hadn't felt since the charges had been brought against her asserted itself, butting her uncertainties aside. She felt new, clean, a shiny coat of varnish over the negative that had colored her life too long. Something that had died had flowered again. She'd added dimension to her life, but she'd reclaimed the old as well. She glanced at the waning moon. "It's morning."

"Yes. Our first day." He shoved open the door, then kicked it shut behind him. His look was solemn. "This is our first moment here. Before counts, but not at this second. All brand-new reactions. New beginnings."

She felt inordinately touched by the special emphasis. This was to be a very special *first*.

The house was cool, air-conditioned against the late-summer heat.

"What do you think?" he asked. "The sitting room is small. The fireplace works. The dining bar between it and the kitchen is new." He jerked his head upward. "That's the stairway leading to the second floor. There used to be three tiny bedrooms. Now there's one bedroom and a bathroom."

"I've been up there. Remember?"

"Yeah. I need to know more."

"What?"

"How you feel."

"I like it."

"Damn! That makes me happy."

She laughed. "Easily pleased, aren't you? Shouldn't you put me down, now?"

"Maybe. Would you like some champagne? I don't chill it, but it's been down in the basement which always stays cold." At her shake of the head he smiled. "I'd rather not waste any time, either."

Arms twined around his neck, she kept her face close to his as he climbed the stairs. Even his pores held interest for her. "Your nose was broken once, wasn't it?"

"More than once. Once by my brothers when we were playing soccer. Once on the soccer field in college."

"Cornell or Harvard?"

"Cornell. My roomie and some others were playing sandlot soccer. I caught an elbow in the nose." He stopped at the entrance to the suite that was at the very top of the stairs. "This is it." He turned so she could see everything.

"Very nice." When he grinned, she chuckled. "Now, don't pretend you were hanging by a thread waiting for my opinion. You know I saw it—"

He kissed her. "First time."

"Right." She was shaking. "Still you weren't wait-ing with bated breath for my—"

"I was, I was. Would've torn everything to pieces if you'd said the word."

"Not true."

"Right. But I'm glad you like it." He kissed her nose, letting her slide down his body. "Would you like to undress me?"

"I thought you were supposed to do that."

"To you?"

"Yes."

"Ma'am, I'd be honored."

Dynasty became more excited just by watching his absorption, his attention to her body. When he looked at her breasts, her nipples lifted and turned pebble-hard. She bit back a groan when he undid her jeans, carefully removing them, then dropping them on the floor.

"Sorry," he muttered. "Should pick 'em up."

"Not to worry. You can press them for me," she said, and laughed through the hot haze that was building inside and around her. Not ever could she recall being so taut, so caught up in passion, yet so unfettered, so . . . so relaxed. Emotions were chok-ing her, but she felt remarkably content. Something must be wrong.

"Stop laughing," he said into her neck.

"I wish I could."

He looked at her. "Would you rather not, Dy-nasty? Your call."

"I would rather, actually. I just feel too relaxed for this to be real."

"That sound you just heard was relief flooding me." He kissed her ear. "It's supposed to be this way, Dynasty. It's never happened to me until now, but I'm damned sure I'm right." He kissed her, taking her lips and her tongue, laving them with his, deepening the kiss to unbearable hunger when her arms tightened around his neck.

Dynasty leaned back. "The air feels good against my skin."

"I like your skin too." He pressed his body to hers. "Wonderful."

"Isn't it?" The smooth abrasion of his nakedness against her sent rivers of pleasure through her. "Umm, you feel good."

"Not as good as you do."

His hoarse voice added impetus to her rising emotions, and she clutched at him.

Lifting her in his arms, he carried her to the bed, placing her on his lap while he tore back the coverlet.

"Careful."

"Yeah." He lifted her up, tossing the cover to the floor. "Don't laugh."

"I can't help it."

He grinned. "So glad you're enjoying this."

"Aren't you?"

His smile faded. "Yes."

She reached up and kissed him. When he pulled her closer, her eyes closed, her body energizing as his hands moved over her.

A new age. Another planet. A crescent of time that had never been traversed. Such were the thoughts coursing through her, until they were silenced by the thunder of passionate need.

Aaron tipped her head up as his descended. A violent hunger was unleashed almost at once. She clutched at him, as though he were the only stability on the planet. She needed his touch, wanted to touch him. She was desperate for the reality he could give her, the life that had been lacking in her world.

Aaron claimed her mouth with a frantic, needy thrust of his tongue. The mating with hers almost unmanned him. He fought for control.

She arched against him, locking her arms around his neck. He pulled her closer, palming her buttocks, groaning at the feel of her soft junction against his aroused body.

He slid his hand to her breast, his fingers outlining her nipple.

"Aaron." His name drifted across her lips as though a breeze carried it.

Hearing the unasked, he bent his head, taking her nipple into his mouth, sucking there. Her head fell back, hanging suspended from her shoulders.

"I want you, Dynasty. What do you want?"

"You."

"Sure?"

"Very."

"You've got me . . . in many more ways than you can figure, darling."

Her fingers dug into him. As though he sensed

the message, his mouth went to her nipple again, pulling her deeply into his mouth, tasting her, possessing her, and giving himself.

He raised his head and looked at her, feverish, intent. They stared at each other long and hard, the power of passion palpitating between them. It was a seal, a bonding they couldn't stop, that went over and around them, creating a oneness neither had dreamed possible.

She touched his face, outlined his mouth, partially open as his breath hissed in and out. "I want you," she said, "if this is desire . . . what I once thought it was, is a poor imitation." She sighed. "I guess I don't want to be one of your many—"

"You're not. You couldn't be." He put his finger on her lips. "I'm the one who made the overtures, offered the commitment. Remember?"

She nodded. "My credulity level is in the basement, Aaron."

"Then think of me as a one-night stand that you can run from, escape if necessary. I'm not, and I have no intention of letting you get away, unless you tell me I'm hurting you." He kissed her cheek. "You're beautiful. I want you."

"Me too."

They sank back on the bed, reaching for each other.

Over and over they kissed, tasting, wanting, not seeming to get enough.

His hands went over her, pausing at her nipples,

bringing them to a pink hardness. "You excite me, pretty lady."

"I—I think you do the same."

Their laughter was short, gasping.

He kissed her throat, the vee at her breastbone, lower, each breast receiving attention. She caught his head. He looked up, eyes unfocused. "What?"

"I need you now," she whispered.

He nodded and moved over her. Inch by inch he entered her. He was large, she, wet and snug. His eyes held hers as he pushed farther. "Dynasty!"

She closed her eyes, biting back a cry. It shouldn't be this good. No elaborate foreplay, but she'd never been so hot.

He began to move; she rose against him, meeting his thrusts with her own. Each one took her breath, the wild, dizzying sensations they evoked driving her on, pushing her over the brink.

As one they entered that long, warm tunnel denied to so many. She climaxed with a groan, her body arching, her hands gripping him.

Sinking his fingers into her hair, he held her firmly, taking her mouth in the same intimate way he took her body. The long, strong culmination was almost more than she could endure.

Burying his face in her neck, he joined her.

They stayed together for long moments. Or maybe it was hours.

❧————❧

Sometime later they rose as one, not speaking, but communicating as though there were words between them.

Side by side, they entered his bathroom. Under the shower, they laved each other, the slow inspection of bodies holding them in thrall.

Their faces wet, strands of hair plastered against cheek and chin, they stared into each other's eyes. They ran their hands over each other. She demanded to know about every scar and mar. He told her, then found a small scar on her. He insisted there was no reason for her to have a mark.

"Roller-blading," she said. "Did it in Manhattan. This one came from roller-skating as a child."

Though her scars were few, he kissed each place where there was the tiniest mark.

She cupped his lower body. It was bold . . . and right. She licked moisture from the base of his throat.

He kissed her behind the ear, smiling when she said it tickled.

He touched her everywhere. "You might be the most beautiful creature in the world."

"I thought horses were the ultimate to a breeder."

He smiled, shaking his head. "You're as pretty as any filly I've had." He grinned when she punched him in the arm.

He finally turned off the water and lifted her from the shower. They dried each other off, then walked into the bedroom again.

Reaching for each other, their mouths searching

and finding, their embraces became urgent, needy. They moved to the bed without speaking.

When the backs of his legs touched the bed, Aaron sat down and pulled her to him, letting Dynasty stand in front of him, between his thighs. He leaned forward, taking a breast into his mouth. "We're building something here, Dynasty. I hope you know that." Each word was spoken between wonderful sucking embraces on her nipples. Waves of red-hot lava took the place of her blood as he flicked her nipple with his tongue.

Her breath came raw and rough. She jabbed her hands through his thick hair, moving his head, but not interfering with his quest down the center of her body. His slight beard brushed her body like sensuous fingers, eliciting new excitement. More, more! Her body felt heavy, achy, damp, flooded with warmth. Her hips began to move.

Aaron splayed each hand over her buttocks, tilting her to his face.

Dynasty gasped, clutching him when she meant to push him away. She couldn't! The promise to never be out of control of her life again seemed to have no validity, though. Giving herself to Aaron made sense. Then she couldn't think. Lost in hazy, burning desire she held on, and wanted more.

He nuzzled her, he kissed the warm triangle of hair.

Then in one strong move, he lifted her onto the bed and followed her. He lowered his head to the cradle of her thighs, kissing her with deep need.

She recognized the keening sound she made. It came from her other self, the one she'd never known, the sensual one who'd been hidden from her all this time. Aaron stroked and instructed with his tongue, probing until she was shaking under him. He sank his mouth into her, and she arched high, a growl coming from her throat.

In sudden rivulets her body released itself into carnal love, and she was initiated into the secrets of all the great lovers of the world.

Aaron pressed into her, caught by her beauty, so enthralled with her passion, he was wild to take her.

In concerted emotion and giving they took each other, holding back nothing.

THIRTEEN

Dynasty woke, blinking, lying still. For a moment she thought she was back in Manhattan. Staring at the ceiling, she tried to remember where she was. Recollection came, and so did her smile. She turned her head, looking at a sleeping Aaron, his hand splayed over her middle. Lying on his stomach, his face inches from her, he looked mussed, sexy, and beautiful.

Leaning forward, she touched his nose with her nose. It quivered, but he didn't move.

Laughing to herself, she eased away from the arm across her and got out of bed to stand naked above him. He was too good to be true. Could love come like that? No man alive had made her feel as Aaron did. She didn't need to make love to him a hundred times to know that he would only get better. She was eager to try out her theory, though. Even thinking about it made her wet. The temptation to jump right back into bed, waken him, and have a go, shook her with mirth and awe. Nothing, no one could have the power of Aaron Burcell. Tiptoeing backward, she kept her eyes on him, smiling, inhaling the remembered pleasures and scent of the man.

She used the bathroom, taking a quick shower. Then she looked at her day-old underwear and grimaced. She couldn't do it. Thinking of how abrasive her jeans would be without underpants had her gritting her teeth. A sudden thought made her smile. Tiptoeing back into the bedroom, she eyed his tall chest. Hoping it wouldn't squeak, she opened the top drawer. Shirts. The second drawer held socks. The third . . . Bonanza! Underwear. It would fall off her, but it would be clean. Her jeans would hold it up. She'd wash them and return them.

She slipped her shirt on, blew the sleeping Aaron a kiss, and left his room.

Unlocking the front door, she stepped out on his porch. An early bird sang high above her. In the distance could be heard the call of a rooster. A buzzing of insects seemed like background music.

Should she go back to the main house for breakfast? She wasn't all that hungry. Inhaling deeply, she pondered her next move. The air was fresh, the slant of coral light in the east told her that the sun would rise in short order. Staying out of doors had great allure.

On impulse, because she wasn't ready for breakfast, and because she wanted to ponder the glorious night just spent with Aaron, being loved over and over again, she turned away from the path to the house. Being fussed over by the house staff didn't set well when all she wanted to do was think of Aaron.

She made a left turn, quite sure it would take her to the stables. Though the lane curved, rose, and bent, it wasn't hard to follow as daylight spread.

When she came to a slight rise, the stable was off to her left. She wasn't surprised to see a great deal of activity. Moving closer, she caught the pungent smell of the stables as the swampers cleaned them. Most of the horses had been let out into a nearby pasture.

Smiles were slanted her way, nods and greetings were given, but work didn't stop. More horses were put out to pasture, others had feed bags attached to them. The everlasting swampers were in and out, heads down, intent, moving fast, but thoroughly.

Dynasty would've like to quiz some of the workers about the horses. Since they were so busy, she decided not to bother them. She wandered around them, through the stable, and out a side door. Across a short walkway was another stable. There was less activity in it. Even to her untrained eye, it looked as though it had been cleaned. There was a fresh odor to it, and most of the stall doors were wide open to catch the air and sun.

She was about to bypass the stable when a movement caught her eye.

At the far end of the stable a man gestured to her, jerked his head right, and pointed to a paper tacked to the stall. When Dynasty walked toward him, he left.

Curious, she ambled to the stall, leaning forward to read the writing.

Dynasty,
The horse in stall three is yours to use. It's best if
you lead him out the side door to the south pasture.
He isn't that friendly to other horses.
A.

Dynasty hadn't thought to ride, but it had appeal. No doubt the animal would be docile and tractable. Aaron knew she was a rank amateur. She looked out the door. The man was not in sight. The sun was rising fast and had become a flaming ball. The sky was an abstract of coral, purple, and cream. Everything seemed brand-new. All at once she was eager to inhale the beauty.

The night with Aaron was so fresh in her mind. Such happiness needed to be celebrated. Wouldn't it be wonderful to ride free across a pasture?

Leaving the note where it was, she moved along to stall three. "Hi."

The horse looked at her. He didn't move toward her, nor did he seem interested in her one way or the other. Reaching up, she took a fresh carrot from the box near the stall. "Would you like one?" She proffered the carrot. Several seconds passed, the horse whinnied and shook his head a few times, then he trotted over to her. She palmed the carrot at him, laughing when he nibbled, then snatched it. Because she was happy and wanted everyone and everything around her to be the same way, she indulged the animal shamefully, feeding him several of the carrots.

"No! No more," she told him, stroking his muzzle. "What's your name? Ah, here it is. Heavens. Where did you get such a Gaelic name? Oengus. If I remember correctly your name is famous in the Irish myths. I have a little of the same blood. We should get along." Moving along to the tack room at the rear, she was stunned at the sizes and shapes of the tack. Carrying a saddle and bridle that most resembled what she was used to, she returned to the stall.

Oengus returned to her at once, bumping her until she gave him one more carrot. "That's enough. Besides that's the last of them." She looked him right in the eye as she lied. He nudged her harder. "All right. So I don't lie well," she muttered. "Do you want to get cramps or develop colic, or whatever it is that horses get? Don't look at me like that. It could happen. Come here, and let me get this on you."

To her relief the horse obeyed.

"Now, come out of there so I can saddle you."

It took minutes of straining, cursing, and perspiring to achieve her aim. "You aren't cooperative," she told the prancing animal. "And don't kick like that. Someone will think you're antisocial."

Swiping a hand across her sweaty brow, she grasped the reins, pushed his stall door wide, and tugged Oengus toward the side entrance. No one was in sight. The meadow looked inviting. She led him over to a mounting block, but it still took her a few minutes to get in the saddle and settle the horse, who seemed intent on sidling and jerking his head.

"Hold it! For heaven's sake, Oengus, you act like you had a burr under your saddle. You don't. I put the damn thing on, so I should know. . . . Hey! Hold it. Better. Now, let's see if we can turn. That's it." Gingerly, she pressed her heels to his flanks, exerting minimal pressure. She was jerked back as the horse surged forward. "Hey! Hold it. I mean, whoa. See if I give you a carrot when we get back."

Thinking she heard shouting, Dynasty turned her head and saw some of the staff waving. She waved back, then had to look around quickly when Oengus started to trot. "Actually this isn't half bad. Your gait is nice and smooth, like Stormy's." When the horse broke to a canter, she froze, then relaxed as she sank into the rhythm of the powerful animal.

Heading down into the meadow was a bit scary, but the view was delightful. Still, beyond the sound of Oengus's pounding hooves she heard more shouting. The staff calling to her, no doubt. She didn't turn, though. Not safe when cantering.

She didn't start to worry until she saw the fence.

"Whoa, Oengus, that's a fence up there. Don't get so close!"

She tried yanking harder on the reins. It didn't slow him down even a bit. In fact, he was picking up speed. "Oh, don't do this. Too fast." Jumping was not in her game plan. Not only had she never done it, she'd never had the desire. "Foolish Oengus! Slow down. Oh Lord."

The shouts behind her were louder now, but Dynasty didn't care. She was hanging on for dear life. "Good Gravy Marie, you're not going to jump that damn thing. Good Gravy . . ." Words died as she gripped the reins with both hands, leaning forward. Where the hell was he going? Just as she started to close her eyes, she felt an arm around her waist.

"Kick free of the stirrups. I have you."

She obeyed. At almost the same moment Aaron lifted her free of the horse's back. Clamped to his side, not quite on him or his horse, she watched Oengus leap high, high, clearing the fence and hedge behind it with grace and tons of room. "Beautiful. I never saw anything like that. How could he—?" Then she heard the crash and the horse scream. "Oh no! What happened?" She clung to Aaron, shaking. "Oh. I'm so sorry. You mustn't destroy him." Tears poured down her face.

"Shhh. It's all right."

"No, it isn't. He—"

"He might be fine. I mean it, Dynasty. Nothing will've happened . . . if we're lucky." Aaron held her close across his saddle.

"You think he's hurt, don't you?"

"I'm hoping his inbred talent will have carried him over." Aaron put his mouth to her forehead. "He's strong. He could've made it . . ." Words died as Rory and one of the stable hands appeared from behind the fence. Rory lifted his hands as though the horse had made a touchdown.

"He's all right?" Dynasty asked.

Aaron nodded, looking down at her. "And so are you, aren't you?"

She nodded. "Were you worried? You shouldn't be—"

"Of course I was. You could've been killed."

Others rode up, silencing her retort.

"Good riding, brother. You should do stunt work in westerns."

"Thanks, Noah." Aaron cuddled her close, turning his horse.

"Wait. I want to see Oengus." Dynasty sensed Aaron's anger. It vibrated against her cheek as she stretched to look over his shoulder. His heart still beat hard, as though it would come through his shirt. He was both furious and fearful. She needed to ask him about that.

"Good job, brother." Terry rode up with her husband. "I haven't seen your trick riding in years."

"And I'd better not see any more for a while," Doogie said, thundering up to them. His horse danced under him as he glared at his son.

"I had to do it," Aaron said.

Doogie nodded. "I know. Oengus would've followed his instincts and gone for it."

"Gone for what?" Dynasty looked from Aaron to his father, frowning. Then her attention was caught by Oengus as Rory led him around the fence. "Oh. Good boy. Are you all right?" She wriggled free of a groaning Aaron and slipped to the ground.

"Don't!" Aaron yelled.

Rory tried to intercept her. She went around him,

reaching for the large head. "Are you fine, big boy?"
She could've cried when she saw the streak of blood
on his neck. "What happened?"

"It's naught a graze from a rambler," Rory said.

"You're not badly hurt," Dynasty told the horse.
"Just a scratch. You're so brave. I can tell it stings.
We'll get something for it. What a good fella you
are." The horse nuzzled her, whinnying, making her
laugh. "Forget that. No more carrots." She was still
patting him when Aaron lifted her from the ground.
"What?"

"I want you away from him."

"That's ridiculous. I was comforting him."

"Let Rory handle him. He's too much horse for
you. You're to give him a wide berth."

"Why? Really, Aaron. You're the one who told
me to ride him."

Silence like a thunderclap settled over the group.

"What did you say?" Aaron asked, his voice just
above a whisper.

"It's the truth, Aaron," Dynasty said for the tenth
time or so.

He didn't stop his pacing. It was all he could do
not to choke on his own heart rate. It had been that
way since she'd made her grand announcement that
he'd told her to ride Oengus. Her sketchy explanation when she'd ridden back with him had seemed
bizarre, too outrageous to be true.

His father and Noah had stayed behind, talking to

the stable hands, searching for the note which they hadn't found when Dynasty had led them to the stable and pointed to the spot. Aaron had told his father he was taking her back to his house. Over and over he had her tell the tale. Each time he became more filled with anger . . . and fear. They were trying to get to Dynasty.

Finally he stopped his pacing. "I know, I know. I believe you." He shoved his hand through his hair. "It's the situation that's so damned incomprehensible. The missing note, the missing man . . ." He stopped when he saw her chin rise.

Striding to her, he hauled her into his arms. "This has nothing to do with trust in you, Dynasty. It's about some damned conspiracy that catches you in the middle." He kissed her hard. "I'd bet my next year's pay it has to do with the horse scam."

"That can't be. I don't know anything about that."

"That's another worry. If this is a move against me and mine, I don't like it. You and my family are in danger. I won't stand for it. Doogie feels as I do. That for some reason you became a target because you mean a great deal to this family." He whitened. "With you hurt . . . or worse, our attention would be off the hunt for our horses and for those who stole and killed them."

Dynasty couldn't lean far back in the tight embrace. She really liked where she was. Safe. "That's far-fetched. Maybe it was because I was in the right place at the right time."

"They knew which member of this family didn't know about Oengus. You're the only one who wouldn't know he'd been a great steeplechaser."

"What?"

Aaron nodded. "He'd been consigned to the pasture after a long and successful career. Rory brought him to this country after hearing about him through a cousin who deals with steeplechasers in Ireland. Rory's a soft touch, like Doogie, so he was only glad to see that the big guy would lead a life of ease." Aaron scowled. "Most of us understand the different temperaments of racing breeds, the needs they have because of their breeding—"

"Jumping," Dynasty whispered.

"Exactly. He's a beautiful horse, but like some steeplechasers, he's temperamental. He can take sudden and long lasting dislikes to people, just ask some of the stable hands." He swallowed. "When I heard you were on him . . . God! Dynasty, don't ever do anything like that again. I damn near died."

"He was very good. He didn't hurt me, Aaron. Truly."

Breath caught in his throat as he crushed her to him. "I couldn't handle it. Can you understand? If I lost you, in any way, it'd be too much. Life would be a void. I'd be empty inside, Dynasty." He stared down at her.

At the anguish in his eyes, her own emotions rose like a flood. Tears came unbidden to her eyes, spilling over and down her face.

He frowned in concern. "You did get hurt, didn't you?"

She shook her head.

"What?" He watched her throat throb as though words stuck there and hurt. "Tell me."

"No one has ever been my protector." Her smile slipped sideways. "Of course my parents were when I was a child. After going to Manhattan and working there, it was hammered home to me that it was every man or woman for himself. No concrete walls to lean on, very slippery ground to stand on." She paused. "I will admit I learned the hard way. When my friends left me at the first sign of trouble, I was hurt, but I learned the lesson of fighting back, surviving." Her lips tightened. "If I hadn't had such a good lawyer, I might've gone down for the count." She looked into his eyes. "She became my friend as well as my defender." She shook her head. "But never has anyone put himself in the line of fire for me as you did today. No one has ever loved or believed in me as you do." Her lips trembled. "It shook me . . . it shakes me."

"Me too. When I saw you on Oengus, heading toward the fences, my heart gave out."

"I don't think so. You rode like a madman. I heard your father tell Rory that. They thought you'd be killed." She cocked her head. "What's behind that fence and hedge, anyway?"

"A damned wide ditch, much like Oengus would be used to in steeplechase racing, only it wasn't as well cared for. Credit to the animal he really thrust on that jump. I think he would've made it as well, if you could've hung on, Dynasty. But how you could have I don't know. Only superior riders take on steeplechasing, and they know the course. You had no idea what was on the other side. I did." He cuddled her close. "I don't want to live through anything like that again."

Resting her cheek against his chest, she tightened her arms around his waist. "You could've been killed."

He smiled into her hair. He understood her fear. "I'm not letting you out of my sight."

She lifted her head. "I must get back to Yokapa County. Dorothy is handling most of the work—"

"And being helped by Pepper, who wants to be more to her."

Dynasty smiled. "I agree. It would be a good match. Pepper is a good man. Strong and full of purpose. They love the country, and love working the land."

Aaron inclined his head. "Will you mind living some of the time in Kentucky?"

She inhaled. "You're taking a lot for granted."

"Because I haven't proposed formally?"

"Because . . . because . . . it might not be right for us."

"You know that isn't true." He put his fingers over her lips when she would've retorted. "Be honest. We belong together."

She kissed his fingers. "We might at that."

"Then consider this. We share our time between New York and Kentucky." He kissed her nose.

"Think long and hard, lady. I don't want to take no for an answer. I don't think I can." He kissed her again. "Get some rest. Food's being brought down here." His smile twisted. "My mother will probably be with it."

"Where are you going?"

"I'm going with my father to the sheriff's office. Your description was sketchy, but better than nothing." He kissed her deeply. "Take a nap. Stay warm."

"I will." He'd kept her heated all through the night. She was beginning to believe he was all she'd ever need.

Aaron held her away from him. "You're a beautiful gutsy lady. And you have a way with horses. Rory says no one has been able to ride Oengus without a great deal of trouble. You managed it with very little. Rory thinks you're in league with the little people. I just think you're a goddess come into my life."

Touched, Dynasty tried to smile. Her lips trembled too much.

Dynasty must have dozed. The slight clatter of dishes, the door closing, and whispers brought her awake. "Hello?"

"Don't get up, dear," Mel said, appearing in the doorway to the living room. "Terry, Clare, Rita, and I have come for a short visit. We won't keep you from your nap."

"Actually, I don't think I need one—"

"You were sleeping when we entered, Dynasty," Terry pointed out.

Dynasty nodded, feeling sheepish, then she stared as Rose, one of the cooks from the main house, began laying out tea and coffee, warm sweet rolls, scrambled eggs, and bagels. "How nice." She reached for a steaming cup and smiled when Rita pushed a plate of tiny sweet rolls toward her. She took one, aware of the eyes on her when she bit into the warm yeasty bread. "Very good." What was going on? Why the committee of four?

"I'll get right to the point."

"Terry!" Mel admonished her daughter, then looked placatingly at Dynasty. "She's impulsive. Slow and easy, Terry, not bashing and crashing."

Alarmed, Dynasty looked from one to the other.

"I don't do that," an affronted Terry said.

"You do," Clare said.

"More like banging and butting, I'd say," Rita added, then subsided with a saucy smile when her sister glared.

"Girls! If you please."

Dynasty straightened, putting down her cup. "Is something wrong?"

"We think you should marry Aaron," Clare blurted out, then grimaced. "Usually it's Terry that's gauche."

"Thank you," her sister said, frost in every syllable.

"You're worse today, Clare," Rita said.

"It wasn't well put, but that's what we mean,

dear," Mel said. "You looked stunned, Dynasty. Hasn't Aaron told you he loves you?"

"He's a fool," Terry said.

"That's not true," Clare said. "He's just slow."

"Clare! Don't disparage your brother that way."

"Right. He isn't slow, he's just not up to par."

"Rita!" Mel sputtered.

Dynasty grabbed her cup and gulped, then coughed as the hot coffee burned her throat.

"Something wrong, dear?"

"Hot," Dynasty gasped.

"Ah. Try the tea."

Dynasty took the cup from Rose, thanked her, and promptly burned her tongue. Miserable, she stared at Aaron's family.

The women started talking at once, defending their positions, calling on times past when one or the other had made gaffes.

Mel finally looked at her. "We've botched it, I think." She cocked her head at Dynasty. "He loves you so much. He needs you. It worries me that you can't love him."

Dynasty's eyes widened. "I can. I do," she blurted.

The Burcell women laughed.

Dynasty frowned at them. "You're all so . . . so . . ."

"Pushy?" Rita suggested.

Dynasty shook her head. "Well armed for living. So sure, so unbeatable."

They laughed again.

Dynasty was a little hurt. "What's so funny?"

"You've described you," Mel said. "My dear, you're a Titan. We all know what you've been through, how you handled yourself in a most trying and frightening situation. You're a credit to your gender, my dear, and I think you've given more than one woman cause to believe that all is not lost when going up against a largely masculine society, such as Wall Street."

Dynasty's smile flashed on and off. "It was hard, but I don't think it was any criteria—"

"You're wrong about that, Dynasty," Terry interrupted. "You fought back, hard. You took them on and proved you were innocent."

"I had a good lawyer."

"Great. It was still your personal courage that carried you through. I never saw anybody go up against the system the way you did and win."

"Terry's right." Clare shrugged. "And I usually don't agree with her."

"Absolutely," Rita said, nodding sharply.

Dynasty felt as though she'd discarded some old and useless luggage as she listened to the Burcell women. "I did have a wonderful lawyer, though."

Terry nodded. "I'm sure it helped. But I saw you on the news, how you kept your head up, how you went back to that court day after day, fighting for your good name." She smiled. "You're so much like Aaron."

Dynasty stared in surprise.

Rita nodded. "Noble. Aar's like that. Maybe that's

one of the reasons he loves you." She bit her lip. "Are you going to let him down?"

"Not your business," Mel interjected.

Dynasty lifted her cup, sipping cooled tea. "He's—he's hard to get rid of."

"Like a burr," Mel said. "His father's that way."

"We'd like you in the family," Rita added. "I suppose that's hardly an inducement to marry Aaron." She smiled. "We could kill off a few."

"Starting with you," Terry said dryly.

"Whatever you decide, dear," Mel said, "we're with you, though I hope you decide on Aaron."

When they left, Dynasty sipped the rest of her tea and pondered the Clan Burcell . . . and Aaron. She finished the tea, put down the cup, and leaned back. Her eyes slipped shut. She was smiling.

FOURTEEN

Dynasty awoke woolly-headed, feeling as though she'd dropped down a deep well. Where was Aaron? A glance at the clock told her she hadn't been asleep that long, though it had been so deep, it'd seemed that way.

Stretching, she surrendered to the restlessness in her mind and let her thoughts have free rein. Why the turmoil? She wondered. Something was eating at her, but she couldn't pinpoint what. Closing her eyes, she emptied her brain as she'd learned to do when studying tai chi. When there was a hollow echo in her mind she turned it loose, opened all doors in the circular area of thinking. Something strove to enter, be seen, be heard. Then it melted away. Taking deep breaths she deepened the emptiness, enlarged the invitation to the unknown. It rattled close, but the picture was blurry.

Opening her eyes, she looked at the phone. She

hesitated, then picked it up and dialed a number from memory. She hoped her old friend would be at his desk. Fortunately, he picked up on the first ring. "Reuben? It's Dynasty . . . Yes, yes, I know it's been ages. I should call more often. Would you believe the berry business takes up a great deal of time? Maybe you could come up this year for Thanksgiving. You could see the place.

"No, I'm not on the farm," she went on in answer to his question. "I'm in Kentucky . . . Yes, there's something on my mind. You're the closest friend I have left on the Street, plus you have a mind like a file cabinet."

"Flattery leaves me unmoved," Reuben said, "but, I'm definitely on your side."

She could hear the concern behind the banter. Reuben Morgenstern was one who hadn't given up on her. He'd spent many hours in the courtroom, sitting right behind her. He'd offered his help to her lawyer countless times. "It could be nothing," she said, then told him all about the theft of Moonstruck, her nearly lethal ride on the steeplechaser, and her suspicions. "I guess you'll have to get back to me," she finished.

"Just tell me where you'll be for the next three days. I'll cover this like a blanket. Trust me."

"I do."

Aaron waited while the phone rang, drumming his fingers on the sheriff's desk.

"Dex Beaman."

"Why the hell don't you answer your phone on the first ring?"

Dex chuckled. "Aaron, old buddy, what's eating you? No one but you barks over the phone in such a charming way."

"Never mind that."

"Trouble?" All amusement had left Dex's voice.

"Plenty." Aaron sketched the recent happenings, omitting any reference to his love for Dynasty.

"Wow! It would seem you're into and onto something. How can I help?"

"Tell me, word for word, how you happened on Dynasty Jones, who told you about the racehorse, what brought the subject up, why was she the target of the conversation."

"Hold on. I'm making notes." Dex paused. "This is a tall order and I damn well don't like the sound of it. Can I get back to you? I want to dig down some and make sure I have everything before I say more."

"Make it quick. I have a bad feeling that my time is limited."

"Aaron expected you to stay until he returned," Mel said to Dynasty.

"I know, Mel, but I must get back. My partner, Dorothy, has had the brunt of the care of the place, and with two of us, it's a full-time job." Besides, Dynasty had the feeling she should be back on the farm when Reuben called. Trepidation crawled over her

skin. If it was something sinister, she couldn't drag
the Burcells into it. They'd had enough with the ter-
rible crimes against their horses. They didn't need to
be involved in something that might be a carryover
from her days on Wall Street. Reuben would set her
straight. Then she'd talk to Aaron. It scared her to
think of facing an unknown alone. It was worse to
dwell on dragging Aaron into it, possibly his family.

"I don't feel right about it," Mel said. She
touched Dynasty's arm. "If you could just wait for
Aaron and Doogie. They should be back soon."

"Don't worry. Please. Tell Aaron I'll call him this
evening." It had been a sudden impulse after talking
to Reuben to leave Burcell Farms. She couldn't rid
herself of the certainty that she was the root cause of
their recent troubles. Arguments with herself, reas-
surances that what had happened to the Burcells preceded her meeting them, did not alleviate the
foreboding, the dark surety that she should leave.

"At least you're letting Rory drive you to the airport."

Dynasty smiled and kissed the cheek of the
woman who'd been the soul of graciousness. How
could she explain her morbid concerns? They were
impossible to discuss.

"You're always welcome here, Dynasty. We've
come to care for you."

"Thank you. You've been more than kind." Dynasty felt teary at the ready acceptance the boisterous
Burcell's had shown her. She really hated to leave. "I
hope I see you very soon, Mel."

The older woman nodded, then watched Dynasty as she went out to the van. She stayed in the doorway until the vehicle was loaded with Dynasty's gear and spinning down the drive. Only then did Mel go to the phone.

"You should've gotten hold of me right away, stopped her," Aaron said to his mother. His anger and frustration showed as his voice rose with each word.

"I tried to stop her." Mel turned to her husband. "Doogie, why did you have to take Aaron with you today? You might've known it would be the day Dynasty wanted to leave."

"How would I know that?" Doogie asked, his tone mild.

"She was agitated."

"Agitated? How?" Aaron fired the questions, then jammed his hand through his hair when his mother's eyes widened. "Sorry. I don't mean to be rude—"

"I know. You love her."

"I do."

"Son, you never said she wanted to go back to New York," Doogie said. "You should've talked to her, convinced her not to go."

"She mentioned she should go back. I thought I had time."

"You should've explained how much safer it would be to remain with us."

"I wanted to keep her here. I didn't want to

frighten her," Aaron said through his teeth. "I thought she'd wait for me. I have to get to New York."

"How about the investigation here?"

"Doogie, I want the situation solved as much as anybody." He shook his head. "But nothing comes before her. Dynasty is my first priority." His eyes narrowed on his father's tight features, his mother's tremulous smile.

"I understand, boy. I'd feel the same way."

Mel nodded. "You keep her safe, Aaron. She's a fine person."

Aaron's smile was fleeting. "She's that and much more. Now, if you'll excuse me, I'm going to see about a flight."

"You won't get one at this time, son," his father told him.

"I'll drive to Louisville and fly out of there in the morning." He ran from the room.

Mel walked over to her husband. "What is it, Doogie? I know you're worried."

He shook his head. "Can't tell right now, honey. Things have gotten a mite blurry." His face hardened. "Maybe this family is in over its head."

FIFTEEN

"What is it, Stormy? You've never been so fidgety before. Tell me." Dynasty tried to stroke the strong muzzle that kept jerking away from her. "Easy, now. I know I've been away for a while, but you know me. I'm your friend."

The horse pulled back from her, rolling his eyes, pawing the ground.

"Easy, easy."

"What's the problem?" Dorothy asked, walking into the barn.

"I don't know. It's not like him to be so jumpy. He was like this when I fed him and the others this morning. I let them out to the pasture but kept him here so I could ride him. Do you suppose he's so fresh that it's made him nervous? He hasn't been ridden in a few days."

"Not a good analogy. He's fresh, but that doesn't tie into nervousness or being edgy. He should be frisky, not acting like this." Dorothy frowned at Stormy. "He didn't seem that fidgety to me yesterday. You saw him yourself last night. He fussed over you when you fed him those apples." Dorothy smiled. "He missed you. That doesn't go hand in hand with being downright skittish."

"He's ill?" Dynasty's heart dropped. "Don't spare me."

Dorothy looked disgusted. "He's the soul of good health. Look at him. He eats like a Trojan. Nothing is expected of him, except an occasional canter to the beach with an inexperienced rider."

"Nice of you to mention that." Dynasty inclined her head. "Are you sure he isn't ill? Thoroughbreds are more sensitive than other horses."

"Sorry. To me he's still a plain old horse. He looks damned good."

"Maybe he's in love." Dynasty chuckled when Dorothy slapped her forehead and asked some deity to keep her from city slickers who didn't know their butt from a barn door. "Well, something's out of kilter."

"I don't think it works that way. His love life would be very effective if we had a mare in heat, I can assure you of that." Dorothy cocked her head. "I thought I heard a truck."

"You have the best hearing. I thought people deafened as they got older."

"In my family we only get better." She gave Dynasty a knowing look. "You've only been home a day. Give him a chance. He'll show up soon."

Dynasty wrinkled her nose. "I didn't think I was so transparent."

"You're not. It's just you can't hide the aura around you. Love has a way of putting a gloss on people that they'd never have otherwise."

"You seemed to have gained quite a sheen yourself."

Dorothy preened. "Yeah. Who would've thought I was so sexy."

Laughter burst from Dynasty. "I would. Okay. You've lifted my spirits. Now, tell me about you and Pepper."

Dorothy blushed, astounding Dynasty.

"We're going to be married. I'm going to keep my place, or sell it to you, and live on Pepper's farm."

Dynasty gave her a big hug. She'd worry how she'd get on without Dorothy later.

"I'm still working for you every day." Dorothy hugged her back.

Dynasty leaned back. "How can you?"

"Easy. Pepper's place runs like a clock. He has all the help he needs, and he's a damned good cook. He's got day help with the house and grounds. It frees me up to do what I like . . . which is working with you on the berries."

Dynasty exhaled. "We're a good team."

"Right you are."

"Now tell me what's wrong with Stormy. I wanted to ride him to the beach, but he seems so fractious, like he's worried or something."

Dorothy puffed out her cheeks, eyeing the horse.

"He's agitated, no doubt about that. I don't think it has to do with you." She shrugged. "He might have a stone in his hoof. I'll take a look."

Dorothy went into the stall, Dynasty at her heels. In slow, sure moves, the older woman went over the horse, cooing to him, talking in low tones. When she was through the two women moved back out to the main area of the stable.

"Nothing there," Dorothy said. "And he is itching about something. Pepper's coming over today to help get the mustangs down to the lower pasture. I'll ask him. He knows a lot about colic and such."

Alarmed, Dynasty jerked on Stormy's halter as Dorothy closed the lower door on the stall.

Stormy reared, whinnying a protest.

"Whoa," Dorothy admonished. "If Lupe comes in here thinking there's trouble, we'll have a circus."

"I know," Dynasty said. "My fault. There you are, sweetheart. Be calm."

Hickory, Dickery, and Doc scampered up the side of one of the other stalls and perched there, eyes on Stormy.

Lupe roared into the barn growling, her head going back and forth, as though she sniffed something unsavory.

"Now, you've done it," Dorothy muttered.

"Oh, Lord. Shh, everybody."

Lupe growled, inching Dynasty sideways.

"Now, stop. There's nothing wrong. All of you, behave." Dynasty's attention went back to Dorothy. "You think it's colic? Isn't that dangerous?"

"I didn't say that. I told you Pepper knew about such things. He'll be here later. Let him do the diagnosing. Don't be jumping to conclusions."

Stormy reared again, this time screeching his ire.

"What on earth . . . ?" Dorothy stared at the horse.

A shadow fell across the front of the stable. Dynasty turned, her mouth falling open as a man lumbered toward her. "You!" She grabbed a pitchfork, but before she could swing it, the man backhanded her, sending her flying.

Lupe leaped, catching the man in the chest.

"Get him off, or I'll shoot him."

"She's a girl," Dynasty said, pushing herself off the ground. She dragged Lupe back by the scruff. Two other men had entered the stable. Why were they at Honeysuckle Farm? "This is private property. Get out of here." The capricious sun slanting into the stable stabbed across the face of the man nearest her. Recognition was reinforced. She gritted her teeth.

"You remember me, don't you, lady?" He grinned, showing a broken front tooth.

"You were at Burcell Farms. You told me to ride the steeplechaser."

"And you did. How the hell you got outta that one, I dunno."

"What are you doing here?" Dynasty asked the man. "You're the reason my horse shied, aren't you? Are you the one who stole him? Abused him?"

"Full o'questions, ain't ya'? Well, I don't answer

'em." He gestured to one of the men, who nodded and left the barn. "But we'll let you talk to someone who'll answer all of your questions."

Aaron's blood went cold when he saw the van. His suspicious nature had been in high gear since he'd flown to Ithaca. The trip from there to Honeysuckle Farm had been the longest of his life.

He managed to get a look at the driver, and did a double take when he saw who was behind the wheel. That he would show himself in Yokapa County revealed a derring-do or desperation that smacked of danger—to Dynasty. Killing the man for threatening the woman he loved was a viable plan.

His call to Dex Beaman while en route to New York had been full of information that Aaron had guessed at, but had hated to know. He'd feared he wouldn't get to Dynasty in time. Calling home, he'd outlined what he was going to do, his hopes and fears. At that moment members of his family were on their way to New York. His argument that they might not be in time, even as he might not be, didn't deter them.

Watching the man he'd known since boyhood, respected for years, Aaron felt a malice rise like a flood. He'd dared to come to Honeysuckle Farm, to frighten Dynasty . . . or worse. At that moment, Aaron longed to confront him, to do him bodily harm for daring to approach Dynasty.

Parked as he was on the neighboring access road

Aaron had a clear view of the van. When he saw someone exit the barn, then go up the lane and wave his arm, his heart sank. Where was Dynasty?

The van moved up the lane and out of sight on the other side of the barn.

After making sure his truck was well covered by thick growth, Aaron climbed out and vaulted the fence that separated the road from Dynasty's south pasture. Keeping low, he crossed the uneven ground at a run. He had to make a wide circuit when he approached the nearer pasture where the mustangs grazed. He talked to them in a soothing murmur. Over and over he reassured them. Where was Moonstruck?

The mustangs danced, shook their heads, but didn't whinny. He made his way down a declivity to a narrow stream, jumped, and climbed up the other side, keeping low. He was almost there.

Reaching the barn, he listened for conversation, anything, that would give him a clue how many there were. He didn't see a guard near the van or outside the barn. If they were that sure of themselves, he had to wonder how long they'd been watching Dynasty.

Edging up, he looked over the lower part of the outer door to a stall. Nothing. Opening it carefully, wincing at the squeak, he melted into the shadows. Holding the door ajar to prevent more noise, he toed around until he found something solid, maybe a road apple. He didn't care. Prop the door. A post-hole digger would have to do.

Taking a breath, he crept over to the stall gate

that opened into the stable area, listening, wishing for a thirty-eight or any other kind of a weapon. His searching fingers found only a pitchfork.

"I'd get out of here if I were you." Dorothy said. "There's a deputy who patrols regularly. He'll stop if he sees your truck. He'll call it in and—"

"Shut up," the man with the broken tooth snarled. "And there ain't been any deputies around this place the last few days. We've checked the traffic around here." He smiled nastily at Dynasty. "We were just waiting for you to get home."

"I was supposed to call my friend, Pepper Lally," Dorothy tried again. "If he doesn't hear from me, he'll alert the police. He's a very suspicious man."

"I said shut up. No more outta you."

Dorothy subsided, glaring.

Dynasty studied the three men from where she stood by Stormy's stall. She couldn't figure out what these men wanted. The one man with the broken tooth had tried to have her injured, or worse, when she'd been in Kentucky. Why? She hadn't known him then. She didn't now. Nor were his companions familiar. Why were they interested in her?

"Why are you here? We've no business with you." She drew in a deep breath, digging her nails into her hands to steady herself. "Get out of here while you can."

"Sorry, we ain't leaving."

"Why?"

"You have something we want. We saw you pick it up. We want it back. Now."

Dynasty shook her head. "I have no idea what you're talking about. Get off my property. On second thought, maybe the sheriff would be interested in you, and why you wanted to kill me by putting me on a half-wild horse."

"It don't matter. You got me in trouble with that foul luck o' yours, lady. I don't mean to let you mess me up this time."

"Oh?" Dynasty flashed a look at Dorothy. She rolled her eyes at Stormy, then looked back at the burly man who faced her. "Don't try anything. This barn is wired to protect us and the horses. You move the wrong way and the siren goes off. See! On the wall."

"We're not stupid, lady," he snarled, though his eyes flashed toward the side of the barn. Just a glance. Enough time to let her snap her fingers at a fretting Stormy's nose. Then she released her hold on his halter. He reared, screaming, reacting to his stung muzzle and, taking exception to the nearness of the broken-tooth man. "He hates you because you hurt him, damn you," Dynasty muttered, fumbling for the pitchfork she knew was somewhere at her side.

Even as Stormy rose, kicking out at the man, Dynasty whirled to confront the other man, who watched the angry horse, mouth agape, his revolver swinging back and forth, as though he sought a target.

Dorothy grabbed her own weapon and rapped the

post-hole digger across the shoulders of the hapless man trying to get away from Stormy. "Dynasty!"

"I'm all right. Did you get him?"

"I coldcocked him with the post-hole digger. How about you?"

"I've got him," she said, holding the man at bay with the lethally sharp pitchfork.

Lupe leaped at the farthest man, knocking him to the ground, slashing and tearing at him, her primeval anger eliciting screams from her victim.

"We've got them," Dorothy crowed. "Whoa, easy boy. Good Stormy. How are you doing, Dynasty?"

"Not bad. If we can shut them up somewhere while we call the police—. Lupe! No. Hold him, girl. Don't eat him. He'd give you indigestion. Slimeball, you're going to jail. No more hurting animals for you. I'm going to call the sheriff and then—"

"I don't think so."

Dynasty turned, her mouth falling open. "You!"

"I thought you would've figured it by now."

Dynasty brandished the pitchfork.

"Don't. I'd just as soon put a bullet in you. Now call off the dog, or he's dead."

"Lupe," Dynasty managed to call. "Come."

Instead of obeying, the dog took umbrage to the new threat to her mistress. She turned and hurled herself at the new intruder.

He fired the gun.

Lupe yelped and fell back, curling into a ball.

"No! Lupe!" Dynasty rushed to the fallen animal.

"Get back, Dynasty Jones."

Lupe was still alive. Dynasty stood and faced the man who had set her up on Wall Street five years ago, the man who apparently wanted her dead. The man the Burcells called a friend. Cal Steelman.

"What are you doing here?" she asked him.

"You've been a thorn in my side for a long time."

"I'm glad."

"You won't be."

His smile shivered over her skin. "Why are you here?" she asked again.

"How the hell did you ever get out of that setup in New York? Your files were salted with information that should've sunk you. It was a perfect plan."

"And you set it up. I was beginning to suspect that. I got a call from a friend this morning who said he'd found some deeply buried inconsistencies about the case against me—and that the smell seemed to come from you."

"Don't talk to me like that." Fury hardened his features.

Sensing a vulnerability, Dynasty pressed forward. "When my friend tied your financial troubles into what I was investigating in my own office before I was charged, he came to some glaring conclusions."

"Who is he?" The question zinged around the barn, reverberating from ceiling to ground in the metal enclosure.

"No one you know."

"Tell me. You wouldn't like the persuasion I'd use."

His cohorts were moving around, groaning, cursing, promising retaliation. Steelman looked at them, then back at her. "We'll table that for now. There's something more pressing."

"And that is?"

"I want what you found that day, Ms. Jones."

She frowned. "I gave you the key ring. Is that what you mean?"

He inclined his head. "It's quite old, in my family for a long time. I was glad to get it back. No. It was important that I found you with it—"

"And you never showed it to Doogie, did you?"

"Of course not. He would've recognized it. Aaron could, too, I suppose. I'm interested in the shell casing. I saw you pick up two things. It was more important I take the key ring then and get the shell later. Those shells are made for a special gun I own and it could have been traced to me. I want the casing."

Lupe moaned.

Stormy reared and screeched, his ears back. Somehow Dorothy had been able to push him behind the stable door, but he was butting it, sounding his fury.

Steelman waved his gun back and forth, eyeing the thoroughbred.

"You're the one who killed Casey," Dynasty said. "And he knows it, doesn't he?"

"Do something about the horse, or I'll shoot him."

"Why?"

For a moment Steelman actually looked frightened. "He wants to kill me."

"I was right."

"It doesn't matter. Do something about him.
Now."

Concealing her horror, Dynasty moved to
Stormy, stepping past a glowering henchman.

Together she and Dorothy heaved and shoved the
horse back so they could latch the stall, keeping him
confined.

"We're between a rock and a hard place," Dorothy said from the side of her mouth.

"I'm sorry you're involved in—"

"Take care of the horse," Steelman ordered,
"then you two stay apart."

Dynasty put her hand over Stormy's muzzle,
hardly feeling the light nips of his teeth as he showed
the temper that roiled in him. Steelman was right.
Stormy did want to kill him. Had he seen Steelman
kill Casey when Casey had tried to save the horse?
Likely. It would seem Stormy had a good memory.
How could that help her? If they did something
they'd surely die. If they did nothing Steelman would
probably kill them anyway. Keep him talking. Cal
Steelman had a very large ego. It'd been pricked
when she'd shown her contempt. Play on it. Think.

Keeping her back to the stall, her hand hanging
over the top, she said, "You tried to kill this horse, as
well as others, and he knows it, doesn't he? It's not
just Clancy you threatened, but Stormy . . . Moonstruck too. How did Rory's father get him away from

you and into the mustang herd? That must've been some trick."

Steelman showed his teeth, a muscle jumping in his cheek. "I knew O'Donal would try to stop me and my men. It would've been better if he hadn't been the one we had to deal with, but he was alone on the outer section of the farm. That was a plus. Several of the thoroughbreds were with him. We just needed one. The plan was to set it up so that if any suspicions arose, Doogie would be the logical choice."

"You're quite good at passing the buck, aren't you?" Dynasty could feel Dorothy's eyes on her. She could only hope Dorothy understood what she was doing.

"You'd do well to keep your observations to yourself, Ms. Jones."

"Casey wasn't the type to go along, was he?"

"He was a fool," Steelman said through his teeth. "I was glad to get rid of him. I needed that horse. When we took Moonstruck he tracked us. How he found the trailer and where we were, I don't know. We were deep in a wild section of my property." His eyes seemed to glaze over with recalled anger. "We were making an exchange of some of my horses there. We were getting ready to trailer Moonstruck when O'Donal moved in. He clobbered two of my handlers and mounted Moonstruck before the others caught on. We chased him down the highway. He knew we were after him. He led us right into a huge roundup of mustangs corralled in holding pens. They were on their way to auctions all over the country. We saw what he did, how he slipped Moonstruck in with the mustangs. There was no way we could cut him loose. He figured he was home free. Cocky bastard. We caught him at a phone. He fought hard." Steelman's laugh was brittle. "He's buried not far from where we killed him."

Dorothy gasped.

It took great effort for Dynasty not to lose her breakfast.

"C'mon, Steelman," Broken-tooth said. "We're wasting time. Let's do it and get outta here."

"Easy, Badger. We're leaving . . . once we protect our investment."

Aaron exhaled slowly. She was keeping him talking. Dynasty was planning something. What the hell did she think she could do against a gun? His blood ran cold when he considered what Steelman could do to her and Dorothy. When Steelman finished his explanations, his ego clock ticking overtime, Aaron would have to make his move . . . and fast. His fingers curled around the handle of a pitchfork. It was all he had. He had to bank on getting Steelman first, surprising the others. Anything to keep them from hurting Dynasty.

"Was it an accident that I bought the thorough-bred?" Dynasty asked.

"Actually it was. When I discovered it, I figured I

could turn it to my advantage. If Doogie couldn't be blamed for the horse stealing, if there was ever a time a patsy was needed, then you'd be the logical one. Everyone knew about your trouble."

"I was exonerated."

Again, his expression hardened with fury. "So you were." His chin came up. "There are still a good many who think you're guilty. It wouldn't take much for me to completely ruin your reputation."

Dynasty reeled. "You vengeful bastard! Because I was innocent, and proved so, you'd involve me in this horse scam. You twisted son—"

"Enough! I don't have to listen to you. You've been trouble for too long. No longer. It's done . . . this day."

Dynasty watched the man as though she faced a cobra. Who could tell what would set him off? His malevolence went deep. He needed to strike at her to assuage some twisted righteousness. Was that her chance? She edged nearer the stall latch. Stormy still snorted his anger. He could be her ace, if she could coordinate all the movements. She eyed Dorothy, who was watching her. A blink was enough.

"Did you lose all your money in the market, Steelman? Is that why you turned to crime?"

"Crime? How can it be a crime when a man quadruples his assets? You're a fool. Not all the thoroughbreds were killed for insurance money, though my underground corporation raked in impressive profits. Some of that money came from selling the most outstanding horses for exorbitant stud fees. What they did with them after, I don't know. I do know there are several thoroughbred farms in this country and Mexico that will flourish in the next few years because they've been able to upgrade the bloodlines of their stock. I've done my part to encourage first-rate breeding."

"How thoughtful," Dynasty said between her teeth. The pompous arrogance of Cal Steelman made her ill. She also knew it wasn't in her best interests to show it.

"It is." His superior smile narrowed to a sneer. "You walked away from your trouble on Wall Street. I didn't like that. You focused the light back on my business when they freed you. Did you know that? Questions were asked. Even when I was able to answer and cover myself, I disliked the spotlight." His face twisted. "You caused it. You, the most miserable of all those twits on the Street that think they know everything. They know nothing. Nothing."

"Hey, Steelman," Badger said. "Knock it off. Let's get on with it and leave. I don't like this."

The gun swung toward the henchmen and back to Dorothy and Dynasty. "Quiet, Badger."

Dynasty closed her eyes for a second, wondering if she'd ever see Aaron again. She was going to fight to stay alive to get to him, to tell him how much she loved him, how precious life would be with him.

Aaron was sweating. Minutes seemed like hours. He chafed at the inactivity, his brain telling him to attack, his love for Dynasty holding him back. Steelman was high enough on anger and frustration to pump a bullet into her before he could get to her. He glanced at his watch in the semidarkness of the stall. By his reckoning, backup was on its way. His father was going to charter a jet, and he and Aaron's brothers should only be an hour behind Aaron.

Aaron shifted slightly, his eyes fixing on Steelman's henchmen. He took deep breaths. They were alongside Steelman now, not spread out as at first. They'd have to be his first target. His gaze moved to Dynasty.

She knew she was in danger. It squeezed his heart how he could read the hand-clenching, mouth-tightening movements. His Dynasty couldn't go down without a fight. It wasn't in her nature to surrender. And that son of a bitch *wanted* to kill her.

Aaron readied himself, still listening. When Dynasty spoke his blood iced over.

"You should leave while you still have the chance, Steelman. Others will figure out what you've done—"

"Hello the barn! Dorothy? Dynasty? It's Pepper. Should I bring the mustangs to the stable? They look fussed about something."

As though the voice was a puppeteer, everyone abruptly moved.

So fast that none could realize what was happening, a quiet Stormy suddenly erupted. Kicking out hard, he broke from his stall, rearing and screaming his rage.

Dorothy pulled a scythe from the wall and hurled it overhand at Steelman. It struck his arm. He screeched as loudly as the horse.

Aaron broke from his hiding place, flinging open the stall door, seeing Dynasty turn as though in slow motion. He didn't stop his charge, look at her or think of anything but the three henchmen. He threw himself at the one with the gun, hoping Pepper would get in there fast and help with the other two.

"What the hell's going—?"

Dynasty heard Pepper's outraged question as she flung herself at the cursing Steelman, who was concentrating on his slashed arm. As before, her hands came up in the curving power of tai chi, and she caught him full on the jaw. Before he could retaliate Dorothy came around the other side of him and punched him.

Stormy was outraged, his hooves pounding the stable as he struggled to get past his rope to the man he hated.

Dynasty struck again, then felt herself flung aside. Dorothy grunted next to her as they tumbled to the stable floor.

"I lost him," Dynasty panted.

"Where did he go?" Dorothy asked, struggling to her feet.

"I don't know. Let's get some more light in here."

"Let's get the horse," Dorothy said. "It looks like our men are handling the rest of it."

Dynasty gripped the horse's muzzle, and felt Dorothy's hands over hers.

"He's not dead anyway, like those other horses," Dynasty muttered, choking back tears. "Aaron?"

"I think he's just fine. . . . Lord! Someone's coming down the drive, lickety-split. Hope it's the police."

Dynasty saw Pepper's silhouette as he lifted one of the henchmen and threw him against the barn wall. The clang and crash reverberated around the two women.

In the golden dust, nothing was really visible except outlines. The noise, though, was earsplitting.

Then suddenly there was silence. The battle was ended.

"Let's open the door," Dorothy said. She and Dynasty threw back the huge front door, illuminating the combatants and revealing a host of men running toward them.

"Who are they?" Dorothy asked, looking around for another weapon.

"The Burcells. All of them, I think," Dynasty mumbled, blinking when Doogie grabbed and hugged her.

"He got away. Steelman," she managed.

"Get him," Doogie said over his shoulder to Noah and Jody. "I want that sucker."

Hands reached past Doogie and pried Dynasty loose. "Dad," Aaron said, "this is Pepper Lally, and this is Dorothy Lesser. And this . . ." He looked down at Dynasty. "This is the woman I'm going to marry. Aren't I?"

"I hope so," she said, grabbing him. When he kissed her she felt a part of herself leave and cling to him. All that had happened in her life had been leading to this. Aaron would be all the reason she'd need to be happy. "I love you."

"Oh, damn," he said, holding her. "Ouch!"

"Oh. I'm sorry. Your jaw is red."

"Dynasty?"

"Yes?"

"Are you really all right?"

"Yes. Are you?"

She nodded. She blinked back tears when he kissed her over and over. Held in his arms, she looked over at Dorothy who was buried in a scowling Pepper's embrace. "Thank you, Pepper."

"I don't like varmints coming here and threatening you and Dorothy," he growled.

"Neither do I," Aaron said, and kissed Dynasty again.

"Pleased to meet you," Doogie said to Dorothy and Pepper. "And Mr. Lally, I'm happy you were here to help Aaron."

Pepper's face creased in a grin. "He wasn't doing too badly. Your son was plenty mad."

Dynasty tightened her arms around Aaron's waist. "I knew you'd come."

"I was damned scared. I heard what Steelman told you." He shook his head. "He was crazy. How could we not know it?"

"Easy," Doogie said. "Like many criminals, he was a great actor."

"He got away," Dynasty whispered.

"He won't get far," Aaron said.

"You knew about Steelman?"

"I got everything on him today, through Dex and some digging."

Dynasty was about to answer when she heard Lupe whine. "Oh. We forgot about her. She's been shot."

"I'll look at her." Pepper disappeared into the barn, then came back out a minute later. "Let's get out of here and get her to the vet. Dorothy, you call the doc from my truck."

They left in a hurry.

"She'll be all right, Dynasty," Aaron said.

Dynasty nodded, glad to be held by him. "We can go to the house. I just want to secure Stormy. He was so brave."

"He knew his enemy. No doubt about it."

Doogie went to the horse, talking to him, calming him. "Good boy."

"He is, Doogie," Dynasty said. "I just knew Steelman must've abused him, otherwise he wouldn't have created a fuss. He's never temperamental."

Aaron chuckled. "There're some on Burcell Farms who'd argue that." His amusement died as they exited the barn. "Where are Noah and Jody? Oh, there they are. . . ." His words died when he saw their expressions. "What?" He tightened his hold on Dynasty.

Noah shook his head.

"Worse thing I've ever seen," Jody said, his voice shaking.

Aaron tried to look beyond them. "Explain."

"What's left of Steelman is out there." Noah jerked his head toward the pasture. "The mustangs got him. Funny. They didn't bother either Jody or me." Noah shook his head. "Maybe they knew what kind of man he was. Trampled the hell out of him."

Dynasty shuddered.

"He brought it on himself," Aaron murmured.

SIXTEEN

It was her wedding day. The cream silk dress was perfect. She stared at herself in the mirror, licking her lips.

It was Thanksgiving weekend. They were having a wedding and the celebration of the national holiday. Maybe next year she and Aaron would be parents. The thought of having a baby in Aaron's image made her reel with happiness.

The door opened behind her, and Dorothy entered. "You look beautiful, Dynasty. I'm so proud of you, and happy for you."

"Why, thank you, Mrs. Lally. I'm glad you and Pepper were able to come down here."

"We like it here," Dorothy said, looking puzzled. "We've been invited down for the races in the spring, and for Christmas . . . and all the other holidays." She blushed. "The Burcells make me feel like family."

"You are. You're my family."

Teary-eyed, Dorothy hugged her. "We work well together."

Dynasty chuckled. "We sure do."

Dorothy studied Dynasty, then smiled. "Never was a prettier bride."

"Thank you."

"When I got married the first time I was already expecting my son."

"Wild woman." Dynasty laughed, then looked thoughtful. "I wouldn't have minded being pregnant today."

"It'll happen soon enough."

"I know."

"Let's go. I heard the organ sounding our cue."

I'm getting married, Dynasty thought. It made her tremble . . . with anticipation. Aaron was her life.

The ceremony had gone as smooth as butter. Dorothy had said that. Dynasty thought it had been a colorful blur. She'd hung simply on to Aaron and kept smiling.

Saying good-bye to everyone was a whirlwind of laughter and good wishes. The next day they'd fly to Los Angeles. From there they'd go to a house on Maui owned by a friend of the Burcells. They'd be alone on a beautiful beach for ten days. Heaven!

"You've been quiet," Aaron said as they walked along the path to his place.

"It's been a wonderful day, full of excitement—"

"Better than that," he said in her ear, scooping her into his arms when they came in sight of the house.

"Caveman."

Aaron shook his head. "Traditionalist. I get to carry you over the threshold, beautiful wife."

"Who loves you," Dynasty whispered as she kissed his cheek, then his ear.

"Take it easy," Aaron warned, his voice hoarse. "I don't have a great deal of control where you're concerned."

"You mean I could get control." She grinned at him.

"Too late. You already have it." He pushed open the door with his shoulder, carried her inside, then kicked the door shut. "Welcome home, Mrs. Burcell."

She clung to him as he carried her up the stairs.

They took a long leisurely shower, loving each other with every laving, whispering love words, talking about their impending trip, about their life.

They dried each other and walked into the bedroom, arms around each other.

Dynasty melted at the hot look in her husband's eyes. "You're all I need, Aaron."

"I love you too. More than you could ever know, Dynasty." His mouth traveled down her neck to her breast, where he became very busy with her nipple.

Aaron sank down on the bed, taking her with him.

He stretched out next to her, their naked bodies touching. "God! Are you as happy as I am?"

"I love you, silly man. Cut the chatter. I want to make love."

"So do I." In slow, tender ministrations he proved it over and over through the night.

EPILOGUE

Churchill Downs was alive with people. It was the Kentucky Derby. The most prestigious race in America was about to take place, and excitement rippled like waves on a shore.

Kentucky had done itself proud. The sun shone. People were dressed in their finery that couldn't possibly outshine the colors that would show on the thoroughbreds led out on the track.

Dynasty couldn't believe Stormy would be racing, that she would watch him compete with other great horses. She was both frightened and exhilarated by the thought. He was more than a horse to her. He was her dear friend who'd protected her. They'd shared some scary moments together. Now he was getting the chance to show his bloodlines, his courage, his great talent on one of the foremost courses of the world.

Aaron put his arm around her, his mouth to her

ear. "He'll do well, even if he doesn't win. He's a champion."

Dynasty kissed him. "I don't want him to fall." She looked over at Dorothy, who raised crossed fingers.

"And they're off!"

Dynasty surged to her feet, grateful for Aaron's supporting arm. It was mind-boggling to watch such unleashed power thundering around the track.

"And they're bunched at the first turn with Wingate's Flurry slightly in the lead. The horse once called Moonstruck and renamed Stormy by his new owner, is at the back of the pack. A great animal, and a sentimental favorite."

Dynasty clung to Aaron, never taking her eyes from the flying horses.

"And around the back turn it's Wingate's Flurry, followed by Apple Dream . . . annnd here comes Stormy. Look at him run—"

"Stormy! Stormy!" Dynasty whispered.

"He's moving up on the outside passing War Bonnet, moving into third place. Apple Dream is taking off . . . And down the stretch they come. Stormy and Wingate's Flurry are neck and neck. But Stormy's forging ahead . . . to the finish line! It's Stormy by a head!"

Dynasty turned in Aaron's arms, crying, laughing. "He did it. He did it."

"You saved him like you saved me, Dynasty. He just showed you how much he loved you. Come along to the winner's circle, Mrs. Burcell."

Eyes shining, she walked at her husband's side, looking back up to the enclosure to wave to Mel and Doogie and the rest of the Burcells who were shouting and laughing.

It had come full circle, she thought. Both she and Stormy had been under a cloud. They'd fought back . . . with the help of friends. No more dark clouds. Not anymore.

As she stepped toward the horse, Stormy whinnied, tossing his head, pushing his muzzle at her. The jockey laughed.

"He always knows you, ma'am."

"We're friends." She patted Stormy's neck. "I guess they can never count us out, big guy."

Aaron kissed her cheek. "Nobody could ever count out Dynasty Jones."

THE EDITOR'S CORNER

Warning: the LOVESWEPT novels coming next month contain large volumes of suspense, heavy doses of hilarity, and enormous amounts of romance. Our authors are professionals trained to provide stirring emotion and irresistible passion. Do try their fabulous novels at home.

A Loveswept favorite for many years and now a rising star in historical romance, Sandra Chastain delights us with a brand-new series, beginning with **MAC'S ANGELS: MIDNIGHT FANTASY**, LOVESWEPT #758. Just when quarterback Joe Armstrong has decided his life is over, the doorbell rings—and a long-legged enchantress makes him reconsider! Annie Calloway insists she isn't a vision or a witch, just someone who cares, but Joe doesn't want his soul saved . . . only a kiss that tastes of paradise. Weaving equal parts heartbreak and humor into a tale of sizzling sensuality and a little magic, bestselling author Sandra Chastain sends a heavenly heroine to the rescue of a wounded warrior who's given up hope.

If anyone knows just how delicious temptation can taste, it's Linda Cajio, who delivers a sparkling, romantic romp in **HOT AND BOTHERED,** LOVESWEPT #759. When he rises from the sea like a bronze god, Judith Collier holds her breath. She'd chosen the isolated Baja village as a perfect place to disappear, but instead finds herself face-to-face with a man whose gaze uncovers her secrets, whose caress brands her body and soul. Paul Murphy makes no promises, offers her only pleasure under a flaming sun, but how can the runaway heiress persuade a tough ex-cop they belong to each other forever? Let Linda Cajio show you in this playfully touching story of love on the run.

No one understands the tantalizing seduction of danger better than Donna Kauffman in **THE THREE MUSKETEERS: SURRENDER THE DARK,** LOVESWEPT #760. Rae Gannon fights back wrenching emotions when she recognizes the man who lay near death in the shadowy cave. Jarrett McCullough had almost destroyed her, had believed an impossible betrayal and shattered her life. But now the untamed mystery man is at her mercy, the air sizzling between them as raw need wars with furious despair. Donna Kauffman demonstrates just how erotic playing with fire can be in this white-hot beginning to her romantic suspense trilogy.

Linda Warren celebrates a love treasured all the more because it has been too long denied in **ON THE WILD SIDE,** LOVESWEPT #761. If she hadn't already tumbled to the track from her horse,

Megan Malone knew the sight of Bill North would have sent her flying! Eight years apart hadn't cooled the flames that sparked between the daredevil jockey and the handsome rebel who will always own her heart. Now, this brash rogue must convince a headstrong lady determined to make it on her own that two hearts are better than one. Praised for her evocative writing, Linda Warren raises the stakes of passion sky high in this wonderful romance.

Happy reading!

With warmest wishes,

Beth de Guzman

Shauna Summers

Beth de Guzman   Shauna Summers

Senior Editor   Associate Editor

P.S. Watch for these fabulous Bantam women's fiction titles coming in October. Following the success of her national bestseller THE LAST BACHELOR comes Betina Krahn's **THE PERFECT MISTRESS**: the story of an exquisite London courtesan determined to make a solid, respectable married life for herself and an openly libertine earl who intends to stay single and free from the hypocrisy of Victorian society; recognized for her sweeping novels of the

American frontier, Rosanne Bittner presents **CHASE THE SUN**: Captain Zack Myers joins the army for one purpose only—to take revenge on the Indians who'd destroyed his world, but Iris Gray longs for the power to tame Zack's hatred before it consumes their love—and even their lives; Loveswept star Peggy Webb now offers her most compelling love story yet: **FROM A DISTANCE** spans the globe from small-town Mississippi to the verdant jungles of Africa with the enthralling tale of one remarkable woman's struggle with passion and betrayal. Be sure to catch next month's LOVESWEPTs for a glimpse of these intoxicating novels. And immediately following this page, check out a preview of the extraordinary romances from Bantam that are *available now!*

LORD OF THE DRAGON

by best-selling author
Suzanne Robinson

The day he was condemned and banished from England, his fellow knights thought they'd seen the last of Gray de Valence. But the ruthless, emerald-eyed warrior had done more than survive in a world of barbaric dangers, he'd triumphed. Now, eager to pay back his betrayers, de Valence has come home . . . only to find his plans threatened, not by another man, but by a volatile, unpredictable, ravishingly beautiful woman. Vowing her own brand of vengeance against the high-handed, impossibly handsome knight, Juliana Welles will do her best to thwart him, to tempt and taunt him . . . until all Gray sees—and all he wants—is her. Yet when a cunning enemy puts their lives in peril, the fearless knight will have to choose . . . between his perfect revenge and the passion of a lifetime.

Juliana threaded her way through the foot traffic on the west bridge—farmers bringing produce, huntsmen, reeves, bailiffs, women bringing dough to be baked in castle ovens. As so often happened, Juliana's temper improved with the distance between her and Wellesbrooke. Once off the bridge, she turned north along the track beside the Clare. She rode in this direction through fields and then woods for over an hour.

Juliana stopped for a moment beside a water-filled hole in the middle of the track. It was as long as a small cart. She remembered splashing through it when she chased after her maid, Alice. A little way off she could hear the stream churning on its way to join the Clare. She would have to turn back soon, but she was reluctant. She still hadn't found the jar containing leaves of agrimony, a plant with spiky yellow flowers. She needed the agrimony, for one of the daughters of a villein at Vyne Hill had a persistent cough.

Clutching her cloakful of pots, Juliana searched the woods to either side of the track for the small white jar. All at once she saw it lying on the opposite side of the path at the base of a stone the size of an anvil. So great was her relief that she lunged across the track. She sailed over the puddle of water, but landed in mud. Her boots sank to her ankles.

"Hell's demons."

Stepping out of the ooze, she picked up the jar, balanced on the edge of the mud and bent her knees in preparation for a jump. At the last moment she heard what she would have noticed had she been less intent on retrieving the jar. Hoofbeats thundered toward her. Teetering on the edge of the mud, she glanced in the direction of the stream. Around a bend in the track hurtled a monstrous giant destrier, pure black and snorting, with a man astride it so tall that he nearly matched the size of his mount. Juliana stumbled back. She glimpsed shining chain mail, emerald silk and a curtain of silver hair before a wall of black horseflesh barreled past her. An armored leg caught her shoulder. She spun around, thrown off balance by the force of the horse's motion. Her arms flew out.

Pots sailed in all directions. Legs working, she stumbled into mud and fell backward into the puddle. As she landed she could hear a lurid curse.

She gasped as she hit the cold water. Her hands hit the ground and sent a shower of mud onto her head and shoulders. Juliana sputtered and wheezed, then blinked her muddy lashes as she beheld the strange knight. He'd pulled up his destrier, and the beast had objected. The stallion rose on his hind legs and clawed the air, snorting and jerking at the bridle. Those great front hooves came down and landed not five paces from Juliana. More mud and dirty water spewed from beneath them and into her face.

This time she didn't just gasp; she screamed with fury. To her mortification, she heard a low, rough laugh. She had closed her eyes, but now she opened them and beheld her tormentor. The knight sat astride his furious war horse as easily as if it were a palfrey. He tossed back long locks the color of silver and pearls as he smiled down at her, and Juliana felt as if she wanted to arch her back and spit.

Juliana scowled into a gaze of green that rivaled the emerald of the length of samite that draped across his shoulders and disappeared into the folds of his black cloak. It was a gaze that exuded sensuality and explicit knowledge. Even through her anger she was startled at the face. It was the face of the legendary Arthur, or some young Viking warrior brought back to life—wide at the jaw line, hollow cheeked and with a bold, straight nose. The face of a barbarian warrior king, and it was laughing at her.

"By my soul," he said in a voice that was half seductive growl, half chuckle. "Why didn't you stand aside? Have you no sense? No, I suppose not, or you wouldn't be sitting in a mud puddle like a little black duck."

Shivering with humiliation as well as the cold, Juliana felt herself nearly burst with rage. The knave was laughing again! Her hands curled into fists, and she felt them squeeze mud. Her eyes narrowed as she beheld the embodiment of armored male insolence. Suddenly she lunged to her feet, brought her hands together, gathering the mud, and hurled it at that pretty, smirking face. The gob of mud hit him in the chest and splattered over his face and hair. It was his turn to gasp and grimace. Teeth chattering, Juliana gave him a sylph's smile.

"And so should all ungentle knights be served, Sir Mud Face."

She laughed, but her merriment vanished when she saw the change in him. He didn't swear or fume or rant in impotence like her father. His smile of sensual corruption vanished, and his features chilled with the ice of ruthlessness and an utter lack of mercy. In silence he swung down off his horse and stalked toward her. Juliana gaped at him for a moment, then grabbed her skirts—and ran.

MARIANA
by Susanna Kearsley

Winner of the Catherine Cookson Fiction Prize

The first time Julia Beckett saw Greywethers, she was only five, but she knew at once that it was "her house." Now, twenty-five years later, by some strange twist of fate, she has just become the new owner of a sixteenth-century Wiltshire farmhouse. But Julia soon begins to suspect that it is more than coincidence that has brought her here.

As if Greywethers were a portal between two worlds, she finds herself abruptly, repeatedly transported back in time. Stepping into seventeenth-century England, Julia becomes Mariana, a beautiful young woman struggling against danger and treachery, and battling a forbidden love for Richard de Mornay, handsome forebear of the present squire of Crofton Hall.

Each time Julia travels back, she becomes more enthralled with the past, falls ever deeper in love with Richard . . . until one day she realizes Mariana's life is threatening to eclipse her own . . . and that she must find a way to lay the past to rest or risk losing a chance for love in her own time.

I first saw the house in the summer of my fifth birthday. It was all the fault of a poet, and the fact that our weekend visit with a favorite elderly aunt in Exeter had put my father in a vaguely poetic mood. Faced with an unexpected fork in the road on our drive home to Oxford, he deliberately chose the left turning instead of the right. "The road less travelled by," he told us, in a benign and dreamy voice. And as the poet had promised, it did indeed make all the difference.

To begin with, we became lost. So hopelessly lost, in fact, that my mother had to put away the map. The clouds that rolled in to cover the sun seemed only an extension of my father's darkening mood, all poetry forgotten as he hunched grimly over the steering wheel. By lunchtime it was raining, quite heavily, and my mother had given sweets to my brother Tommy and me in a vain attempt to keep us from further irritating Daddy, whose notable temper was nearing breaking point.

The sweets were peppermint, striped pink and white like large marbles, and so effective at hindering speech that we had to take them out of our mouths altogether in order to talk to each other. By the time we reached the first cluster of village shops and houses, my face and hands were sticky with sugar, and the front of my new ruffled frock was a stained and wrinkled ruin.

I've never been entirely certain what it was that made my father stop the car where he did. I seem to remember a cat darting across the road in front of us, but that may simply have been the invention of an imaginative and overtired child. Whatever the reason, the car stopped, the engine stalled, and in the ensuing commotion I got my first watery glimpse of the house.

It was a rather ordinary old farmhouse, large and square and solid, set back some distance from the road with a few unkempt trees dotted around for privacy. Its darkly glistening slate roof sloped down at an alarming angle to meet the weathered grey stone walls, the drab monotony of color broken by twin red brick chimneys and an abundance of large, multipaned windows, their frames painted freshly white.

I was pressing my nose against the cold glass of the car window, straining to get a better look, when after a few particularly virulent oaths my father managed to coax the motor back to life. My mother, obviously relieved, turned round to check up on us.

"Julia, don't," she pleaded. "You'll leave smears on the windows."

"That's my house," I said, by way of explanation.

My brother Tommy pointed to a much larger and more stately home that was just coming into view. "Well, that's *my* house," he countered, triumphant. To the delight of my parents, we continued the game all the way home to Oxford, and the lonely grey house was forgotten.

I was not to see it again for seventeen years.

That summer, the summer that I turned twenty-two, is strong in my memory. I had just graduated from art school, and had landed what seemed like the perfect job with a small advertising firm in London. My brother Tom, three years older than myself, had recently come down from Oxford with a distinguished academic record, and promptly shocked the family by announcing his plans to enter the Anglican ministry. Ours was not a particularly religious family, but Tom jokingly maintained that, given his name, he had little choice in the matter. "Thomas Beckett! I ask you," he had teased my mother. "What else could you expect?"

To celebrate what we perceived to be our coming of age, Tom and I decided to take a short holiday on the south Devon coast, where we could temporarily forget about parents and responsibilities and take advantage of the uncommonly hot and sunny weather with which southern England was being blessed. We were not disappointed. We spent a blissful week lounging about on the beach at Torquay, and emerged relaxed, rejuvenated, and sunburned.

Tom, caught up on a rising swell of optimism, appointed me navigator for the trip back. He should have known better. While I'm not exactly bad with maps, I *am* rather easily distracted by the scenery. Inevitably, we found ourselves off the main road, toiling through what seemed like an endless procession of tiny, identical villages linked by a narrow road so overhung by trees it had the appearance of a tunnel.

After the seventh village, Tom shot me an accusing sideways look. We had both inherited our mother's Cornish coloring and finely-cut features, but while on me the combination of dark hair and eyes was more impish than exotic, on Tom it could look positively menacing when he chose.

"Where do you suppose we are?" he asked, with dangerous politeness.

I dutifully consulted the map. "Wiltshire, I expect," I told him brightly. "Somewhere in the middle."

"Well, that's certainly specific."

"Look," I suggested, as we appraoched village number eight, "why don't you stop being so pig-headed and ask directions at the next pub? Honestly, Tom, you're as bad as Dad—" The word ended in a sudden squeal.

This time, I didn't imagine it. A large ginger cat dashed right across the road, directly in front of our car. The brakes shrieked a protest as Tom put his foot to the floor, and then, right on cue, the motor died.

"Damn and blast!"

"Curates can't use language like that," I reminded my brother, and he grinned involuntarily.

"I'm getting it out of my system," was his excuse.

Laughing, I looked out the window and froze.

"I don't believe it."

"I know," my brother agreed. "Rotten luck."

I shook my head. "No, Tom, look—it's my house."

"What?"

"My grey house," I told him. "Don't you remember, that day the cat ran onto the road and Daddy stalled the car?"

"No."

"On the way back from Auntie Helen's," I elaborated. "Just after my fifth birthday. It was raining and Daddy took the wrong turning and a cat ran onto the road and he had to stop the car."

My brother looked at me in the same way a scientist must look at a curious new specimen, and shook his head. "No, I don't remember that."

"Well, it happened," I said stubbornly, "and the car stalled just here, and I saw that house."

"If you say so."

The car was running again, now, and Tom maneuvered it over to the side of the road so I could have a clearer view.

"What do you think it means?" I asked him.

"I think it means our family has bloody bad luck with cats in Wiltshire," Tom said. I chose to ignore him.

"I wonder how old it is."

Tom leaned closer. "Elizabethan, I should think. Possibly Jacobean. No later."

I'd forgotten that Tom had been keen on architecture at school. Besides, Tom always knew everything.

"I'd love to get a closer look." My voice was hopeful, but Tom merely sent me an indulgent glance before turning back onto the road that led into the village.

"I am not," he said, "going to peer into anyone's windows to satisfy your curiosity. Anyway, the drive is clearly marked 'Private'."

A short distance down the road we pulled into the car park of the Red Lion, a respectable half-timbered pub with an ancient thatched roof and tables arranged on a makeshift terrace to accommodate the noontime crowd. I stayed in the car, preparing to take my shift as driver, while Tom went into the pub to down a quick pint and get directions back to the main road.

I was so busy pondering how great the odds must be against being lost twice in the same spot, that I completely forgot to ask my brother to find out the name of the village we were in.

It would be another eight years before I found myself once again in Exbury, Wiltshire.

This time, the final time, it was early April, two months shy of my thirtieth birthday, and—for once— I was not lost. I still lived in London, in a tiny rented flat in Bloomsbury that I had become rooted to, in spite of an unexpectedly generous legacy left to me by my father's Aunt Helen, that same aunt we'd been visiting in Exeter all those years earlier. She'd only seen me twice, had Auntie Helen, so why she had chosen to leave me such an obscene amount of money remained a mystery. Perhaps it was because I was the only girl in a family known for its male progeny. Auntie Helen, according to my father, had been possessed of staunchly feminist views. "A room of your own," Tom had told me, in a decided tone. "That's what she's left you. Haven't you read Virginia Woolf?"

It was rather more than the price of a room, actually, but I hadn't the slightest idea what to do with it. Tom had stoutly refused my offer to share the inheritance, and my parents maintained they had no need of it, being comfortably well off themselves since my father's retirement from surgical practice. So that was that.

I had quite enough to occupy my time, as it was, having shifted careers from graphic design to illustration, a field I found both more interesting and more lucrative. By some stroke of luck I had been teamed early on with a wonderfully talented author, and our collaboration on a series of fantasy tales for children had earned me a respectable name for myself in the business, not to mention a steady living. I had just that week been commissioned to illustrate a sizeable new collection of legends and fairy tales from around the world, a project which excited me greatly and promised to keep me busily employed for the better part of a year. I was on top of the world.

Ordinarily, I'd have celebrated my good fortune with my family, but since my parents were halfway round the world on holiday and Tom was occupied with Easter services, I had settled for the next best thing and spent the weekend with friends in Bath. On the Monday morning, finding the traffic on the main road too busy for my taste, I detoured to the north and followed the gentle sweep of the Kennet river toward London.

It was a cool but perfect spring day, and the trees that lined the road were bursting into leaf with an almost tropical fervor. In honor of the season, I drove with the windows down, and the air smelled sweetly of rain and soil and growing things.

My arthritic but trustworthy Peugeot crested a small hill with a protesting wheeze. Gathering speed, I negotiated a broad curve where the road dipped down into a shallow valley before crossing over the Kennet via a narrow stone bridge. As I bumped across the bridge, I felt a faint tingling sensation sweep across the back of my neck, and my fingers tightened on the wheel in anticipation.

The most surprising thing was that I wasn't at all surprised, this time, to see the house. Somehow, I almost expected it to be there.

I slowed the car to a crawl, then pulled off the road and stopped altogether, just opposite the long gravel drive. A large ginger cat stalked haughtily across the road without so much as glancing at me, and disappeared into the waving grass. Three times in one lifetime, I told myself, even without the cat, was definitely beyond the bounds of ordinary coincidence.

Surely, I reasoned, whoever owned the house wouldn't mind terribly if I just took a casual peek around . . . ? As I hesitated, biting my lip, a flock of starlings rose in a beating cloud from the field beside me, gathered and wheeled once above the grey stone house, and then was gone.

For me, that was the deciding factor. Along with my mother's looks, I had also inherited the superstitious nature of her Cornish ancestors, and the starlings were a good luck omen of my own invention. From my earliest childhood, whenever I had seen a flock of them it meant that something wonderful was about to happen. My brother Tom repeatedly tried to point out the flaw in this belief, by reminding me that starlings in the English countryside were not exactly uncommon, and that their link to my happiness could only be random at best. I remained unconvinced. I only knew that the starlings had never steered me wrong, and watching them turn now and rise above the house I suddenly made a decision.

Five minutes later I was sitting in the offices of Ridley and Stewart, Estate Agents. I confess I don't remember much about that afternoon. I do recall a confusing blur of conversation, with Mr. Ridley rambling on about legal matters, conveyances and searches and the like, but I wasn't really listening.

"You're quite certain," Mr. Ridley had asked me, "that you don't want to view the property, first?"

"I've seen it," I'd assured him. To be honest, there seemed no need for such formalities. It was, after all, my house. My house. I was still hugging the knowledge tightly, like a child hugs a present, when I knocked on the door of the rectory of St. Stephen's, Elderwel, Hampshire, that evening.

"Congratulate me, Vicar." I grinned at my brother's startled face. "We're practically neighbors. I just bought a house in Wiltshire."

DON'T MISS THESE FABULOUS
BANTAM WOMEN'S FICTION TITLES